One of the *apaches* groaned as he began to regain consciousness.

Clint drew his pistol and aimed it at the thug's face. Marcel kicked the man in the ribs.

"Who sent you?" the Gunsmith demanded, cocking his revolver to accent his demand.

The man stared up at him fearfully.

Marcel snapped an angry sentence in rapid French. The *apache* replied in the same language.

"He says he and his comrades were paid five dollars each to take care of us," Marcel told Clint.

"Just how were they supposed to take care of us?" the Gunsmith asked.

"Fatally," Marcel replied. "It would appear Lacombe is prepared to take this war to its ultimate conclusion."

"Kill or be killed." *Some vacation!* Clint thought.

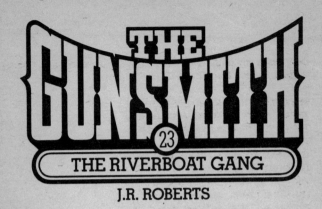

THE GUNSMITH

23

THE RIVERBOAT GANG

J.R. ROBERTS

CHARTER BOOKS, NEW YORK

THE GUNSMITH #23: THE RIVERBOAT GANG

A Charter Book/published by arrangement with the author

PRINTING HISTORY
Charter Original/December 1983

ISBN: 0-441-30894-5

Charter Books are published by The Berkley Publishing Group,
200 Madison Avenue, New York, N.Y. 10016.
PRINTED IN THE UNITED STATES OF AMERICA

Dedicated to Paul Glen Neuman

ONE

The French call it *déjà vu:* the mysterious sensation that one has experienced something before. However, Clint Adams knew the trip on *La Reine Rouge* had evoked a familiar feeling for a perfectly natural reason which had nothing to do with psychic phenomena.

Clint had traveled on a riverboat bound to New Orleans once before. That had been years earlier in 1873, when the government had enlisted him for a simple mission—at least, it was supposed to have been simple. President Grant had needed a small package delivered to a man named Paul Martel and Clint had been chosen to act as courier.

And why had Washington selected Clint Adams for this task? Because he was better known as the Gunsmith, a title unwittingly acquired from a newspaperman who had used it to add color to a story about a young deputy sheriff in Oklahoma. Clint served as a lawman for eighteen years before he resigned to become a genuine gunsmith. He generally traveled throughout the West in his wagon which served as both home and shop. His constant companion and only partner was Duke, a big black Arabian gelding—eight hundred pounds of strength, speed, intelligence and loyalty.

1

However, the Gunsmith was famous not for his ability to repair and modify firearms but for his unbeatable lightning fast draw and uncanny accuracy with a gun. His reputation frequently got him into trouble and his skill was usually required to get out of it.

As he stood on the aft deck of *La Reine Rouge*, watching some fishermen in a boat in the distance haul up their nets, he reflected on the reasons for his current trip to New Orleans. This time the government hadn't sent him on a mission. The trip had been Clint's idea.

During his previous visit to New Orleans, the Gunsmith hadn't had time to enjoy one of the most colorful and exciting cities in the world. Still, he'd seen enough of New Orleans to recognize its potential. Now, years later, he'd decided to withdraw a thousand dollars from his savings and return for a short vacation to make the most of his second visit to New Orleans.

Clint had boarded *La Reine Rouge* at Galveston and rode along the Gulf of Mexico instead of traveling down the muddy Mississippi.

The Gunsmith went below deck to check on Duke in the stable hold. He found the horse in a stall. Duke whinnied a greeting as Clint approached and extended his muzzle to be patted and scratched. Clint obliged, stroking the Arabian's long muscular neck as he entered the stall.

"How you doing, big fella?" he asked, locating a brush which he applied to the horse's glossy black coat. "This sure as hell is better than traveling by rail, isn't it?"

Duke whinnied enthusiastically and bobbed his head as if to agree. A young Negro hostler, in charge of the stable, stared at the horse with disbelief.

"Lord ha' mercy," he whispered. "That feller's atalkin' at his hoss and the critter done answers him!"

"Yeah." Clint smiled at the hostler. "I figured he'd agree with me. Some folks claim a horse can't remember very much, but no one will ever convince me that Duke here doesn't have one long accurate memory. He didn't object when I led him up the gangplank of *La Reine Rouge* and took him to this hold. But if I'd taken him to a locomotive, Duke would have snorted and pawed the ground like I was escorting him to a torture chamber."

"Is that a fact, suh?" the hostler asked, gazing at Clint as if he doubted the man's sanity.

"Sure is." The Gunsmith nodded. "You see, we once rode in a train from Brownsville to Yuma. Duke had to travel in a cattle car located near the engine and he had to put up with a lot of soot and smoke. He remembers all that filth and grime on the train trip, but he also recalls our first journey to New Orleans on board the *Mississippi Queen* a few years ago. He likes traveling by boat."

"If'n you say so, suh." The hostler bobbed his head. "Reckon I'd better go topside and see if'n they needs me for anythin'. 'Scuse me, suh."

Clint made certain Duke had enough to eat and drink. He brushed the gelding and talked to him for a while before he draped Duke's personal hand-woven Navajo blanket over the animal's broad back.

"You have a good night's sleep, big fella," Clint urged. "I'm going to see if I can't manage to convince some of those fellas in the casino to make a contribution or two to my billfold."

Duke snorted in reply.

"Aw, come on." The Gunsmith sighed. "I usually do pretty well at cards. I'll be careful not to drink too much and—"

Duke looked at him and exhaled through his teeth.

"Critic," Clint muttered. "Well, we're going to have fun in New Orleans, boy. There won't be any trouble this time."

Duke snorted again.

TWO

The Gunsmith hadn't expected much from the casino. *La Reine Rouge* was large and ornate, but only a boat nonetheless. There's a limit to the room available on any vehicle and Clint assumed the riverboat would concentrate on using space for carrying cargo and passengers.

But Clint didn't know *La Reine Rouge* means *The Red Queen*.

When he entered the casino, Clint discovered how wrong his assumption had been. A lush red carpet covered the floors and the walls were covered in velvet. Crystal chandeliers hung from the ceiling and the furniture consisted of walnut tables and chairs.

The casino featured a long bar with a leather-topped counter and a well-stocked supply of bottles on the shelves behind it. No patrons stood at the bar, but stewards dressed in white dinner jackets shuffled back and forth from the counter to the gambling tables, carrying trays of glasses and beer mugs.

They make it easy to get drinks in here, Clint was thinking. That figured. Liquor makes men careless with their money. They bet too boldly and tend to be distracted easily. The Gunsmith realized a gambling house does what it can to put the odds in its favor. Plenty of available liquor is one way for the house to get an edge.

Did *La Reine Rouge* casino resort to other methods—such as employing card cheats for dealers?

The Gunsmith glanced over the games of chance and decided this wasn't likely. The casino had a roulette wheel and a dice table, and the main card game appeared to be baccarat. All of these games put the odds in the favor of the house and the place was crowded with enough customers to guarantee a big profit while keeping the games honest.

Clint was surprised to see so many patrons. On his previous riverboat trip he'd played poker, but the games had been relatively modest and the setting far less exotic. The Gunsmith felt a bit out of place, dressed in his denim shirt, Levi's and stetson, because everyone else in the room wore silk shirts, suits and ties.

"Hey, cowboy!" a voice called.

Clint turned to see four men seated at a circular table. A portly figure dressed in a blue business suit, a derby perched on his head, pointed at Clint with a fat cigar jutting from between his fingers. The Gunsmith approached the table.

"You talking to me, friend?" he asked.

"That's right, cowboy," the man answered with a grin. "We've got us a poker game in progress. You interested?"

"I'm interested," Clint replied. "But I'm not a cowboy."

"Well, have a seat and tell us who you are then," the fat man urged. "I'm Fred Nells from Shreveport."

Nells tilted his round head toward the tall gaunt man dressed in a black suit with a high, starched collar who sat to his left. "This is Mr. Dancer."

"*Danzer,*" the cadaverous man corrected, his voice

rolling out the word slowly. Clint wondered if Danzer was an undertaker. If he wasn't, he should have been.

"I'd better introduce myself before Nells mispronounces my name as well," a card player with a well-waxed cowhorn mustache declared. "Name's Thurgood Mandel of Mandel, Richardson and Summers, attorneys at law in St. Louis."

"I'm Clint Adams," the Gunsmith replied. He'd noticed a bulge under Mandel's left arm. The lawyer carried a gun in a shoulder holster beneath his frock coat. "Pleased to meet you fellas."

"And I am Roger Lacombe," the fourth man at the table stated as he shuffled a deck of cards. He didn't bother to look up. "Now, if we've finished with the social graces, perhaps we can get back to the game, *oui?*"

Clint sat at the table while Roger began to deal the cards. He glanced at the surly Lacombe. He was a young man, well dressed in a velvet suit with black lapels and a ruffled white shirt; Roger's lean, angular face may have been handsome if a sneer hadn't been frozen on his lips. The Gunsmith noticed Roger's hands as Lacombe shot the cards across the table to the players. They were soft hands with long slim fingers adorned with diamond rings and capped by manicured nails. Lacombe was certainly a man of means and apparently unaccustomed to work of any kind.

Lacombe explained the rules of the betting in the game. "One dollar ante. You meet the bets or go elsewhere and play for matchsticks with old men."

"Where are the old men?" Nells commented after he picked up his cards and examined them. "Had me a run of luck earlier, but I reckon it petered out for now. I fold."

"Fold," Danzer said sourly.

"I'm in," Mandel declared happily. "I'll take two cards and bet you twenty."

Roger looked at his cards. "I'll see your bet and raise you twenty." He barely glanced at the Gunsmith as he added, "Adams?"

Clint checked his cards. Two queens, the eight of clubs, the eight of spades and the king of diamonds. "I'm in. One card."

He discarded the king. Roger dealt the fresh cards to the players still in the game. Clint glanced at Mandel and saw the man draw a turnip-shaped watch from a vest pocket. Mandel consulted his timepiece and shrugged. Nells struck a match and lit his cigar stump.

"Adams . . ." Fred Nells mused thoughtfully. *"Clint Adams?* You wouldn't be the fella they call the Gunsmith, would you?"

"Like you said, Mr. Nells," Clint replied dryly, *"they* call me that. I call myself Clint."

"The Gunsmith?" Lacombe frowned.

"Mr. Adams is a famous man," Mandel explained as he put his watch away. "He's a gunfighter. Said to be the fastest draw in the West. Faster than Wyatt Earp or even Wild Bill Hickok, so they say."

"No one was faster than Bill," Clint told him as he picked up his new card.

"You should know," Nells remarked. "I understand you and Hickok were supposed to be pretty good friends."

"Yeah," the Gunsmith replied simply.

"There's nothing wrong with earning your living with a pistol," Lacombe stated. "Providing you're good at it."

"I'm not a gunfighter," Clint told him.

"Have it your way, Adams." Roger shrugged. "I raise the bet forty dollars."

"I'll see you and raise fifty," Mandel announced.

Clint had a good hand, but not an unbeatable one. Did Roger or Mandel have a better hand? Mandel seemed pretty confident, but he could be bluffing. Roger Lacombe's expression revealed nothing except apparent boredom and smug contempt. A perfect poker face because it was too annoying to study very long.

The Gunsmith mentally shrugged. *That's why it's called gambling,* he thought.

"I'll see your bet," Clint announced. "And call."

"Call," Lacombe confirmed.

"Full house." Mandel smiled, placing his cards face up on the table.

The lawyer had three fours and two kings. The Gunsmith noticed one of the cards was the king of diamonds. Lacombe grunted and tossed his hand on the table. He'd been playing a bluff with a pair of jacks. Mandel's smile spread across his face until Clint placed his cards on the table.

"Some full houses are better than others," the Gunsmith remarked. He had three queens and two eights.

"Your pot, Adams." Lacombe sighed, passing the deck to Mandel.

Thurgood Mandel chatted about his last visit to New Orleans as he shuffled the cards. Clint ignored the lawyer's chatter and concentrated on the man's hands. Mandel dealt everyone five cards. The Gunsmith looked at his hand. Three jacks, a queen and a ten. He put them face down on the table.

"Pass," he said.

Mandel looked at him with surprise. Nells and Danzer also passed. Lacombe and Mandel again raised bets with each other. The lawyer finally called.

"Two pair," Roger Lacombe declared, putting his queens and nines on the table.

"Full house." Mandel grinned as he showed his cards. The attorney had three kings and two aces.

Lacombe frowned at Mandel as the lawyer raked in the pot. Danzer dealt next, but Clint still kept an eye on Mandel. The Gunsmith had decided the man was probably not from St. Louis and was certainly not an attorney. Mandel continued to babble away, asking the other card players about their reasons for making the trip. Once again, he consulted his turnip watch. New cards were dealt and Mandel returned his watch to a vest pocket.

When Clint checked his hand, he could hardly believe what he had. His face didn't betray him as he listened to Mandel make the first bet. Clint, Lacombe and Nells met it while Danzer folded.

"Two cards," Nells said.

"One," Lacombe stated.

"I'll go with my hand," Mandel told them.

"So will I," Clint said.

Danzer dealt Nells and Lacombe new cards. Mandel raised the bet. Nells and Lacombe passed.

"I'm in," Clint announced. "And I raise you one hundred dollars."

"Oh?" Mandel smiled. "Pretty sure of yourself, eh?"

"You said it, friend," Clint agreed, tossing cash into the kitty. "Meet the bet or pass."

"I'll see you." Mandel nodded. "And I raise you another hundred."

"You've got it," Clint confirmed, adding more money to the pot. "Call."

Mandel smiled and displayed his hand. "Full house," he announced. "Aces high."

The Gunsmith placed his cards face up on the table. The

nine, ten, jack, queen and king of spades stared up at the startled Mandel.

"Flush," Clint said as he reached for the kitty.

The ominous click of a gun hammer being thumbed back filled the Gunsmith's ear as a hard metal tube jammed into his left temple. Roger Lacombe had a .41 caliber Remington derringer pressed against Clint's head.

"Cheating at cards is a capital offense on board *La Reine Rouge*," he hissed.

THREE

The card players rose from the table and backed away as Clint slowly moved his hands from the pot and raised them to shoulder level. Lacombe still held the derringer at his head.

"You should never accuse a man of anything unless you have proof, Roger," the Gunsmith remarked in a toneless voice.

"This game has smelled bad ever since you sat down with us, Adams," Roger declared.

"The stink was already here. You guys just didn't notice it before."

"*Monsieur* Lacombe," a steward cried. "*Que faites-vous, monsieur?*"

"*C'est un cochon,*" Roger said, gesturing at Clint with his derringer. "*Il est tricheur, oui? Comprendez-vous?*"

"I understand you say this man is a card cheat, *monsieur,*" the steward said. "If that is true, then let us deal with him."

"*If* it is true?" Roger snapped. "Of course it is true! Do you dare call me a liar, Debray?"

"No, *monsieur,*" Debray assured him. "But it is our job to handle such matters."

"I caught this *tricheur,*" Lacombe declared. "I will deal with him!"

"*Monsieur*, your brother will not approve."

"I will worry about Gaston," Roger insisted.

"Right now I'm only worried about you, friend," Clint Adams remarked. "Since you're the fella with a gun aimed at my head. Before you kill me for another man's sins, why don't you ask Mandel what time it is?"

"*Qu'est-ce que c'est?*" Roger frowned, his Remington still aimed at Clint's head. "What do you mean by that, Adams?"

"He's trying to wiggle out of this—" Mandel began.

"You've got a holdout card in your vest, Mandel," Clint explained. "You've been plucking high cards out of your pockets throughout the game. I knew you were cheating when I discarded the king of diamonds, which somehow found its way to your hand. Then you dealt me three jacks to try to trick me into betting high so you could win back your losses. That's why I folded on the second hand."

"That's a lie!" Mandel cried.

"You probably cheated the last time too," Clint continued. "But you didn't cheat well enough to beat the hand Lady Luck gave me."

"The lady isn't smiling on you now, Adams," Lacombe warned, but he'd moved his derringer from the Gunsmith's head. "However, we'll see who is telling the truth. Empty your pockets . . ."

Roger pointed his gun at Mandel. "*Both* of you!"

"Jesus," Mandel rasped. "I'm not a card cheat!"

"Then empty your pockets," Lacombe instructed.

The incident had attracted the attention of everyone in the casino. A crowd formed around the poker table. Dozens of eyes watched Clint, Mandel and Roger move away from the table. Lacombe put away his derringer as two stewards joined him. They opened their white jackets to reveal the walnut butts of revolvers thrust in their belts.

"Check Mandel's vest pockets," Clint advised.

"All right," the "lawyer" began, reaching for his vest.

Suddenly, Mandel's hand dove inside his jacket and yanked a .32 Smith & Wesson from its shoulder holster. The stewards clawed at their weapons. Lacombe recoiled fearfully and tried to draw his derringer, but Mandel's S&W was already in his fist. He turned the pistol toward Lacombe.

The gunshot boomed like a dynamite explosion in the confines of the room. Thurgood Mandel's body twisted about violently, blood spurting from his right shoulder. The S&W flew from the man's fingers. He grasped his wounded shoulder with his left hand and sunk to his knees.

Everyone turned to stare at the smoking Colt .45 in the Gunsmith's hand. Clint calmly holstered the revolver.

"You guys want to check his vest pockets now?" the Gunsmith inquired dryly.

Lacombe glared at the dazed form of Thurgood Mandel who still knelt on the floor, clutching his bullet-shattered shoulder. Roger spat something in French and stepped forward to unleash a vicious kick. The heel of his shoe smashed into Mandel's mouth hard and sent the card cheat sprawling across the floor.

The steward called Debray knelt beside the unconscious Mandel and searched his pockets. Debray rose and handed a fistful of cards to Roger Lacombe. Tossing the pasteboards aside, Roger jerked his head toward the exit door. Debray and another steward grabbed the senseless Mandel and dragged him out of the casino.

"What are they going to do with him?" Clint asked Roger.

"Never mind," the Frenchman snapped. "Just be

thankful *you* are not about to face the same fate, Adams!''

''What the hell are you talking about?'' the Gunsmith demanded.

''You should have told me about Mandel as soon as you saw he was cheating!'' Lacombe snarled.

''I can understand a man making one mistake,'' Clint sighed as he strolled closer to Roger. ''But you just made a second one. . . .''

Without warning, he smashed his fist into the point of Lacombe's jaw with enough force to knock the Frenchman to the carpet.

''You failed to apologize for accusing me of cheating and pointing a gun at me,'' the Gunsmith explained.

A hard metal object jammed into the small of Clint's back. The Gunsmith stiffened as the steward cocked the hammer of the gun pressed against Clint's spine. Another steward plucked the .45 from the Gunsmith's holster.

''*Cochon!*'' Lacombe growled as he sat up and wiped a trickle of blood from his mouth. ''*You* have made a serious mistake yourself, Adams.'' He drew his derringer once more. ''A *fatal* one!''

FOUR

"Stop!" an authoritative voice boomed.

The stewards immediately lowered their weapons and turned to face the speaker. Roger Lacombe scowled, his body trembling with rage. Clint Adams winced when he saw the derringer wobble in Lacombe's fist. He hoped the hotheaded Frenchman wouldn't pull the trigger by accident.

"Roger!" the commanding voice snapped. *"Mets de côté le pistolet—immediatement!"*

Reluctantly, Roger Lacombe lowered his Remington. The crowd parted like the Red Sea for Moses as two men strode across the casino toward the Gunsmith.

Clint raised his eyebrows with surprise. A short, portly man dressed in a purple smoking jacket, silk pajamas and slippers strolled toward him. His attire would have seemed amusing if everyone present hadn't treated the little man with such fearful respect.

Clint doubted that anyone regarded the man lightly. He walked with slow, arrogant majesty. Louis the Fourteenth had probably strolled through his court in just such a manner. The man was obviously accustomed to being in charge. He was entirely confident of his authority and power in that casino.

A tall muscular figure followed the little king. The big man wore a gray suit, his shirt open at the throat and a dark

16

blue beret perched on his head. He limped slightly, dragging his right foot as he walked. Yet nothing about the man suggested weakness. Muscles strained the fabric of his clothes at the shoulders and chest. The man's face was as hard as seasoned walnut, his eyes black diamonds. A Smithers shotgun with sawed-off barrels and a cut-down stock hung from a shoulder strap by his right hip.

"I told you to put that gun away, Roger," the portly man said in a firm, deep voice. "How many languages must I use before you do so?"

"This bastard hit me," Roger complained, but he pocketed his derringer.

"Is that so?" the monarch turned to face Clint. "And why did you do this, *Monsieur*—?"

"Adams," the Gunsmith replied. "Clint Adams."

He explained what had happened and why he'd struck Roger. The little king nodded.

"I apologize for my brother's rash behavior, *Monsieur* Adams," he told Clint. "I am Gaston Lacombe, the owner of *La Reine Rouge* . . . and other things that produce a worthwhile profit."

"A pleasure to meet you, Mr. Lacombe," Clint replied. "I can't say I'm all that happy about knowing your brother."

"You may call me Gaston," the senior Lacombe said, his tone suggesting this was a great honor for the Gunsmith. "I have some excellent French brandy, *monsieur*. Could I interest you in joining me for a glass?"

"Sure can, Gaston." Clint nodded. "Just let me get my winnings."

The Gunsmith raked up the money he'd won at the poker table and hastily stuffed it into his pockets. He wasn't sure how much he had, but it was a hell of a lot more than he'd started the game with.

Gaston and his hulking companion escorted the Gunsmith from the casino. They walked through a corridor until arriving at the door of a private cabin. Clint noticed the door was hand-carved in red oak. The big man opened it for Gaston and his guest.

Clint resisted the urge to whistle when he saw the room within. The cabin was a plush office with a large walnut desk, two oil paintings on the wall and a tin ceiling which reflected the light of two kerosene lamps mounted on the walls.

"*Merci*, Jules," Lacombe told his towering servant. "*Deux verres eau-de-vie, s'il vous plaît.*"

"*Oui, monsieur.*"

Jules headed for a mahogany liquor cabinet, shuffling his right foot along the carpet. Gaston moved to his desk and sunk into a leather armchair behind it.

"Please be seated, *Monsieur* Adams," he invited, gesturing at a chair in front of the desk.

"Call me Clint," the Gunsmith urged as he accepted his host's offer.

"Of course, Clint." Gaston nodded. He reached for a wooden humidor. "Would you care for a cigar?"

"No, thank you," the Gunsmith declined.

Jules lumbered forward, carrying a silver tray with a crystal decanter and two balloon glasses. He placed the tray on the desk and poured brandy into each glass, carefully putting equal amounts in the snifters. Then he moved away from the desk and stationed himself at a corner like a well-trained dog awaiting orders from its master.

"Please excuse Roger," Gaston began as he plucked a cigar from the humidor. "He is young and rather rude. A familiar combination these days, eh?"

Clint shrugged. "I don't think your brother and I are going to be exchanging Christmas gifts this year."

Gaston lit his cigar and puffed gently. "You're a man of the world, Clint. Catching a card cheat as you did, you must be quite clever and observant. A man of many skills, *oui?*"

Clint simply shrugged once more.

"Of course," Gaston began slowly. "I would expect nothing less from the Gunsmith."

"I get the impression you want something, friend," Clint mused, sipping his brandy.

"I'm always interested in a man with your talents," Gaston replied as he blew a gray circle of smoke toward the ceiling. "I could use a man like you, Clint."

"I'm not looking for a job, Gaston," the Gunsmith told him. "I'm on vacation."

"Being French, I believe a man should blend pleasure with business," Lacombe remarked. "And business with pleasure, *oui?*"

The door opened. Gaston looked up and smiled as the scent of lilac perfume drifted into the room. Clint Adams glanced over his shoulder and saw a tall, shapely figure clad in a black gown with a diagonal gold slash extending across its front.

The woman may not have been the most beautiful Clint had ever seen, but she must have ranked among the top five. She stood tall and erect. Her hair was jet black and bound into a bun held in place by a diamond stickpin. The woman's features were classically beautiful with a wide sensuous mouth, a compact nose and large gray-blue eyes. Clint, always a gentleman, rose as the lady entered the room.

"I heard a gunshot, Gaston," the girl began. "Is there a problem?"

"Nothing that Clint Adams couldn't handle for us," Lacombe assured her, gesturing at the Gunsmith.

"Monsieur Adams." She nodded at Clint.

The woman studied the Gunsmith's face, noticing the jagged scar on his left cheek which marred his otherwise handsome features. Somehow the scar seemed to enhance rather than detract from Clint's rugged good looks.

"You have the advantage, ma'am," the Gunsmith said. "I don't know your name."

"Ah," Gaston declared. "This is Baccarat, my ward, so to speak."

"Baccarat?" Clint raised his eyebrows.

"Correct, *monsieur,*" she confirmed. "If all is well, Gaston, I believe I shall return to my cabin now."

"I'd rather you didn't go back alone, dear," Lacombe told her. "Clint? Would you mind doing me a favor and seeing Baccarat to her room?"

"It'd be a pleasure, Gaston," the Gunsmith replied.

FIVE

The Gunsmith followed Baccarat along the corridor. She seemed to glide gracefully across the floor as she walked. She was probably the most elegant female he'd ever met. All of which made Baccarat extremely attractive and intriguing, but not the least bit trustworthy. The Gunsmith was suspicious of her convenient interruption at Gaston's office.

But what sort of game might Lacombe and his "ward" be playing?

"Well, Clint thought, *so far it's been pleasant enough. Might as well enjoy it until I find out what they're up to.*

The girl led Clint to her cabin and handed him the key. He unlocked the door and opened it for her.

"Thank you, *monsieur."* She smiled. "Would you care to have a glass of wine before going to bed?"

Clint nearly made a hasty comment in response to "going to bed," but he merely grinned and nodded.

A kerosene lantern mounted on the wall illuminated the cabin. Light was reflected by the tin ceiling, which was decorated with paintings of pink cherubim. The room was definitely feminine with expensive ivory-white furniture and delicate porcelain statues and a lush sky-blue carpet.

Baccarat slipped an arm into the crook of Clint's elbow and escorted him to a cream-colored loveseat. Then she moved to a liquor cabinet and extracted a decanter of red wine from a shelf. The girl sat beside him and poured the scarlet liquid into two goblets, giving the Gunsmith a much larger portion than herself.

"Tell me about yourself, *monsieur*," she urged.

"First of all," the Gunsmith began, "I prefer to be called Clint. I'm more curious about you. How'd you come by a name like Baccarat?"

"Gaston christened me with that title," the girl laughed. "You see, he won me at a baccarat table."

"Won you?" Clint stared at her.

"Of course," Baccarat replied. "I was raised in an orphanage—a rather unprincipled orphanage, I'm afraid. They discovered they could make a greater profit by selling certain children to special types of private enterprise than they could make by dealing with individual families."

"White slavery?" the Gunsmith asked, startled by her tale.

"Not quite an accurate description," Baccarat answered. "I was pretty and appeared older than I was, with a good mind and a promising body. A successful New Orleans madame considered me an ideal candidate for her academy. I received a good education which concentrated on music, manners and the arts of pleasing a man's every need. I was trained to be a first-rate lady of the evening."

"Must have been pretty rough," Clint remarked.

"Not as bad as wandering the streets and eating other people's garbage," Baccarat remarked. "It could have been a lot worse. Someone *always* has it worse, if you just look around a little."

"That's one way to look at it, I guess. But you said Lacombe won you?"

"At a baccarat table." She nodded. "You see, Madame Monique sold me to Sam Holden, the owner of the second to largest cannery in Louisiana. He wasn't a bad sort when he was sober. However, Sam seemed to spend most of his time getting drunk. He was drunk the night he and Gaston met at that baccarat table in the Cheville casino. Anyway, Sam lost all his money so he bet me . . . and Gaston won."

"What's your real name?" the Gunsmith asked.

"Baccarat is as good a name as any," the girl said with a shrug. "I've told you the story of my life, now tell me something about yourself."

"Not much I care to talk about," Clint told her. "I'm taking a vacation in New Orleans. There was a disturbance in the casino and a fella got a bullet in his shoulder."

"You didn't kill him?"

"I didn't say I was the one who shot him."

"Gaston wouldn't have called you into his office unless he had a reason. My guess is you must have revealed quite a prowess as a pistolman to get his attention, Clint."

"*My* guess is you already knew about the shooting," the Gunsmith told her. "And *you* wouldn't have invited me into your cabin unless you had a reason either."

Baccarat frowned. "The moment I met you I knew this silly game wouldn't work."

"Lacombe knew Mandel had been wounded before he entered the casino," Clint began. "A couple of the card players had already referred to me as the Gunsmith and I figure Debray and the other steward probably overheard that. They probably told Gaston I'd shot Mandel. Lacombe figured he'd try to enlist me into his flunky army. So he told you to wait awhile so he could make his sales pitch. Then you arrived just in time, right?"

"So you've got it all figured out." She sighed.

"And I'm not interested in working for Lacombe," Clint declared. "I can't see myself waiting on him hand and foot as if he was the king of Siam. Maybe Jules doesn't mind, but it's not my style."

"Sounds like you've made your decision, Clint," Baccarat remarked. "I won't try to change your mind. You've probably got the right idea. Nobody should belong to Gaston unless they have no other choice."

"And you don't have any other choice?" Clint inquired.

"I'm Gaston's property." The girl shrugged. "That doesn't leave me much choice about anything."

"You could leave him," Clint told her.

"You don't know Gaston," she replied.

"I don't think I want to."

"He can be a generous man," Baccarat explained. "But he never surrenders anything that belongs to him and nobody ever walks out on Gaston. Besides, where would I go? I've been trained and raised to serve only one function. If I wasn't Gaston's mistress, I'd belong to someone else just like him."

"You could start over somewhere else," the Gunsmith suggested. "A person can always change his or her life if they really want to."

"You have to stay alive long enough to try," Baccarat stated. "But before you go, I'd like to ask a favor."

"Ask," he urged. "All I can say is yes or no—and I'll say yes if I can."

"Well, I was instructed to go to bed with you to try to influence your decision," she explained. "I know you won't change your mind, but I'd like to go to bed with you, anyway."

The Gunsmith's eyes widened with surprise. "That's the favor you want?"

"Sex has usually been a duty for me," Baccarat told him. "I'd like to enjoy it for sheer pleasure. I know it would be that way with you, Clint."

Why me? the Gunsmith wondered, but he didn't openly question his good fortune. The woman was beautiful and very exciting. She was exotic, appealing and intelligent, yet rather sad.

Sad, that is, assuming she'd told Clint the truth. Did the lovely Baccarat have a trick or two up her figurative sleeve? The Gunsmith had known enough female vipers to realize they could be just as dangerous and even more cunning than their male counterparts. He recalled the deceitful Tiffany Case, the murderous Sofia Mendez and the conniving Abby O'Shea. Baccarat could be another gila monster in disguise, but she was too damn beautiful and sexy for the Gunsmith to ignore her offer.

He moved closer and slipped an arm around Baccarat's trim waist. The girl embraced his neck and their mouths crushed together in a passionate, hot kiss. Tongues slithered and probed. Their hands slowly slid across shoulders and backs. The girl's fingers traced Clint's jawline, sending erotic signals along the facial nerve while his equally skillful touch found the small of her back and massaged her spine.

They gradually increased the foreplay. Baccarat unbuttoned his shirt and reached inside to slide a hand across his hairy chest. The Gunsmith's fingers groped at her breasts, gently rubbing the nipples until they stiffened under his touch. Clint kissed her neck, running the tip of his tongue along the hollow of her throat.

Baccarat gently broke the embrace and rose to slip the

straps of her gown from her shoulders. She tugged at the
dress and it slid down her long, lean frame to fall in a
bundle at her ankles. Baccarat wore nothing underneath.

The Gunsmith's gaze traveled over the woman's naked
beauty. Her figure was flawless. Baccarat's swanlike
neck seemed to extend directly to the swell of her large
globular breasts. Her slender waist and rounded hips were
mounted on long shapely legs. Clint's desire for her
burned within his loins as he rose and hastily stripped.

The girl was equally pleased with the Gunsmith's
physique. Tall and lean, Clint seemed larger without
clothing due to the muscular development of his shoulders
and chest. His body was not that of a boy. The Gunsmith
had seen more than forty summers and survived numerous
encounters with violence. Scars from bullets and knives
marred his flesh, yet like the facial scar, this only contrib-
uted to the Gunsmith's masculinity and made him all the
more attractive to Baccarat.

They moved to the bed. The Gunsmith sat on the edge
of the mattress and pulled the girl into his lap. He kissed
Baccarat's breasts, teasing the bare nipples with his teeth
and tongue. His hand fell to her thighs, stroking the warm,
soft flesh.

Baccarat purred with pleasure. She kissed his neck and
nibbled at his earlobe. Slowly, she slid from his lap and
lowered her face to Clint's crotch. Baccarat's lips brushed
his rigid manhood. Her tongue traced the head of his
penis. The Gunsmith sighed in contentment as she took
him in her mouth.

The girl expertly drew on Clint, riding her lips up and
down the length of his shaft. Clint's nerves tingled with
pleasure as she continued to suck his hard throbbing
manhood.

The Gunsmith felt himself near his limit. Baccarat, with the instinct of a woman adept at lovemaking, realized this and slid her lips from Clint's erection. Then she lay on her back, lovely long legs parted wide.

Clint lay beside her. Their lips met once more. He groped at the dark triangle between Baccarat's thighs, inserting two fingers into her. The girl moaned happily as he probed deeper, moving his hand to and fro.

Then he mounted her. She found his hot, stiff cock and guided it home. Clint sighed as he sunk into the warm, wet sheath of flesh. He gradually worked himself into her womanhood. The girl bounced beneath him, drawing Clint deeper. The Gunsmith responded eagerly, pumping his member again and again.

Baccarat gasped, her nails biting into his shoulders. Clint increased his thrusts, faster and harder. She cried out in ecstasy and convulsed as an orgasm swept through her. Clint continued to ram himself inside the girl. This time they rode to glory together. His organ exploded its seed as she withered in a second climax of delight.

"God, that was good," Baccarat purred as she snuggled against Clint's chest.

"You're quite a woman," he replied, stroking her hair gently.

"Not really," she whispered.

"Don't argue with me," the Gunsmith told her. "I happen to be a great judge of women. A regular *connoisseur* as the French would say."

"I like you, Clint," Baccarat said. "So I'll give you some advice. When you leave this room, avoid Gaston and everybody associated with him . . . including me. Gaston can be trouble. The sort of trouble that can get you killed."

SIX

The rest of Clint's voyage aboard *La Reine Rouge* proved uneventful. He avoided the casino and the Lacombe brothers. Twice he saw Roger arrogantly strolling along the deck with some of the bodyguards dressed in steward uniforms. The young Lacombe glared at Clint, but he also steered clear of the Gunsmith. Apparently Gaston had warned his brother to keep away.

The Gunsmith also noticed Jules limp from the passenger section to relay some orders to other members of the crew, but he didn't encounter Gaston Lacombe or Baccarat again. Another person Clint didn't come upon was Thurgood Mandel. No one had mentioned the missing card cheat or speculated—aloud—about what had happened after the stewards dragged him out of the casino. The Lacombes clearly dealt out their own brand of justice aboard the riverboat.

Clint was relieved when *La Reine Rouge* finally arrived at New Orleans. He gathered up his belongings and led Duke down the gangplank, eager to put some distance between himself and the Lacombe brothers. Clint regretted his inability to somehow help Baccarat, but there seemed to be little he could do for a girl who had learned to accept her fate as part of the natural order of her life.

The Gunsmith headed for the French Quarter. Clint steered Duke around wagons and carriages as he rode through the cobblestone streets. Magnificent buildings with ornate balconies and stained-glass windows flanked both sides of the road.

Crowds milled about the streets. Businessmen in suits and construction workers clad in overalls and caps moved along the sidewalks. Housewives examined vegetables, fruits and fresh fish displayed on the stands in the marketplace. Bakery shops offered bread and pastries, and clothing stores sold a wide selection of garments, ranging from work clothes to silk and linen finery.

Clint located a livery and paid the local hostler handsomely to give Duke the very best care. Satisfied he was leaving Duke in competent hands, the Gunsmith left the livery and checked into the Royal House, an exquisite hotel nearby.

"*Oui, monsieur?*" a pinch-faced desk clerk inquired, giving Clint's clothing a fish-eyed look of disapproval. "May I help you, sir?"

"Sure can," Clint replied, dumping his saddle and bags on the wine-colored carpet of the hotel lobby. "I'd like a room."

"The Royal House is a bit expensive, *monsieur*," the clerk explained. "A room here is five dollars a day. True, you may well find this outrageous, but I do not make the prices. Perhaps you will be happier elsewhere. May I suggest—"

"I'll be staying here for approximately six days," the Gunsmith told him, peeling bills from his billfold. "Okay if I pay thirty-five dollars in advance to cover an entire week in case I decide to stay over a day or two?"

"Oh!" the startled desk clerk nodded. "*Oui, monsieur*. We will be honored to have you as a guest, *monsieur*—?"

"You can read it in the register as soon as I finish

signing in," Clint told him as he gathered up a quill pen from the desk. "How about a key?"

"Of course," the clerk assured him, turning to a row of boxes on the wall behind him. "Room twenty-three is very nice, although it offers little in the way of a view from the window. For an extra dollar a day . . ."

"I'm not going to pay extra just to be able to have something pretty to look out the window at," Clint told him. "I'd rather take something pretty up to my room instead, if you catch my drift."

"But of course, *monsieur.*" The clerk smiled. "I am, after all, French, *oui?*"

"Uh-huh." The Gunsmith nodded. "And I'm hungry."

His nostrils twitched as the aroma of freshly prepared food drifted from the dining room. The clerk handed Clint the key to his room.

"Do me a favor, friend," Clint began. "How about keeping an eye on my saddle while I go get some grub? Reckon that eatery over yonder oughta have some red-eye and vittles, don't it?"

"I'm certain you'll find our dining hall has *something* that will appeal to you, sir," the clerk assured him, once again apprehensive about having the Gunsmith for a tenant.

"And you'll look after my saddle for me?" Clint thought about running a finger under his nose, but decided not to overact.

"*Oui . . .* yes, sir," the clerk agreed reluctantly.

"Hell, thanks partner," Clint declared, swinging his saddle over the counter to the man. "Surely do appreciate this. That chunk of leather and me done shared many a hemorrhoid. That's a joke, old son."

"Oh, yes." The clerk nodded, handling Clint's saddle

as one might a diseased corpse. "Very amusing, sir."

"I do admire a fella with a sense of humor," the Gunsmith said, giving the man a dollar. He'd decided that he'd upset the clerk enough to get even for the man's snobbish attitude.

"Oh, *thank* you, sir!" the clerk said with surprise.

"That's Western hospitality, friend," Clint shrugged.

He walked to the dining room. The maître d' met him at the entrance, escorted the Gunsmith to a table and summoned a waiter who gave Clint a menu and filled his water glass. The Gunsmith began to examine the menu when he noticed a woman seated alone at a nearby table.

She displayed a wide smile to reveal that Clint had caught her eye as well. He tilted his head toward the empty chair across from his. The girl nodded, rose and walked to his table. Clint got to his feet and helped the lady with her chair.

"A gentleman," she mused with approval.

"It's easy to be a gentleman when one meets a beautiful woman," the Gunsmith replied.

Indeed, she was lovely. Although barely five feet tall, the girl had a perfectly proportioned hour-glass figure. Her curly red hair was clipped a bit too short and her smile seemed a bit artificial, but otherwise she was quite lovely and charming. The Gunsmith passed her the menu.

"I'm getting the lobster creole," he announced.

"An excellent choice," she said. "I'll have the same. My name is Sheryl. With whom am I dining?"

"Clint Adams," he replied. "What would you favor? Champagne or white wine?"

"Champagne, of course." She smiled. "Are you staying at the hotel, Clint?"

"Yeah," the Gunsmith answered, wondering if Sheryl was a whore. He noticed she wore a lot of cheap costume jewelry, and judging from her dark brown eyes, he guessed she'd dyed her hair bright red.

The Gunsmith never paid a woman for her affections, but the subject of paying for pleasure didn't come up during their conversation. Sheryl didn't say much about herself. Neither did Clint, yet the conversation remained pleasant enough.

After dinner the pair mounted the stairs. Clint glimpsed an ominous figure between the balusters. A burly black man, well dressed in a blue pinstripe suit and derby, glanced up at him and hurried away. The Gunsmith's hand hovered close to the grips of his holstered Colt. New Orleans was a rough city and Clint knew lots of gangs of hoodlums operated in the French Quarter. These ranged from remnants of the old Bonaparte extremists to the Italian Mafia. Crime has no color barrier. Some of the gangs consisted of black hoods.

However, Clint and Sheryl reached the head of the stairs unmolested. They located room twenty-three and Clint unlocked the door. He struck a match and lit the kerosene lamp on a table in the center of the room while the girl closed the door.

"Nice room," Sheryl remarked.

"Yeah," he agreed glancing about with approval. "It is."

The floor was covered by a dense green carpet and the walls were papered dark blue. The furniture was far less spartan than the hotel rooms Clint was accustomed to. The furnishings included a loveseat, a desk, a chest of drawers and a four-poster bed.

"That's nice too," she commented, indicating the bed.

Sheryl approached Clint. He placed his hands on her shoulders and lowered his mouth to hers. The kiss was long and lustful. Their tongues wiggled across each other within the caverns of their mouths. Sheryl's hand slid across Clint's chest and slowly moved lower until it touched the bulge at his crotch.

She slowly sunk to her knees before him and unbuttoned Clint's trousers. His hardened manhood jutted from the gap. Sheryl ran her tongue along the length of his penis. Her lips slipped over the fleshy head and gradually moved up the shaft.

Clint gasped as Sheryl's head bobbed, her mouth riding his swollen member from tip to root. She increased the speed of her motion, drawing her lips firmly around his stiff cock. The Gunsmith whispered her name to warn the girl that he was nearly at the brink, but she ignored him and continued to suck his maleness even faster.

Clint groaned as his penis spewed its load into Sheryl's mouth.

She accepted his seed and continued to milk his cock with her lips. The Gunsmith trembled as the girl expertly drained him before releasing his manhood. Sheryl swallowed his load with relish and smiled up at him.

"How's that for a start?" she inquired.

Before Clint could reply, he heard a man cry out for help, mingled with the sound of fists smacking into flesh. The Gunsmith bolted to the window and yanked back the curtain. He gazed through the glass pane to see three figures thrashing about in the shadows of the alley below.

Two young muscular men were methodically beating the hell out of a gray-haired man. The goons had pulled down their victim's suit jacket to bind his arms with the garment. They hammered their fists into the senior man, driving him to a corner in the alley.

"Jesus!" Clint rasped, drawing his Colt from leather.

"Don't!" Sheryl cried.

Clint turned to assure her she was in no danger. He saw

the door open. The burly black man Clint had noticed at the stairs stepped into the room. He held a diminutive .31 caliber "baby" dragoon pistol. However, the black guy took one look at the big .45 in Clint's fist and immediately dropped his puny weapon and raised empty hands overhead.

"Don't shoot, mister!" he cried.

"I—I don't know this man, Clint," Sheryl said nervously.

The Gunsmith glanced at the door and noticed a lace handkerchief on the floor. Sheryl had obviously marked the door with the cloth when she'd closed it, thus letting her partner know which room to go to for their intended target. Clint clucked his tongue with disgust.

"I don't have time to waste with a couple of petty shakedown artists," he growled. "Get out of here. Both of you!"

Sheryl and the black man hurried from Clint's room. The Gunsmith heard the man snarl, "Bitch." The clap of a palm striking a cheek was closely followed by Sheryl's yelp of pain. Clint ignored the would-be thieves and turned his attention to the murderous scene in the alley below.

Unless he acted quickly, an old man was about to be beaten to death right before his eyes.

SEVEN

The Gunsmith yanked open the window and climbed onto the balcony beyond. The two thugs were still punching their helpless victim. They allowed the gray-haired man to sag and fall to the ground. Then the pair began to kick him in the torso.

"Stop!" Clint Adams shouted, aiming his revolver over the rail of the balcony, pointing it at the figures below.

One of the muscle boys woodenly raised his hands in surrender. The other man reacted by executing a fast whirl, drawing a pistol from his belt. Clint caught a glimpse of gunmetal as the thug swung the weapon toward the Gunsmith.

Clint squeezed the trigger of his Colt. The big revolver bellowed. An orange muzzle flash lit up the alley below for a flickering of an instant. The Gunsmith saw the startled, fearful face of the hoodlum at the very instant his nose exploded when the bullet smashed through it into his brain.

The second hoodlum quickly dove for the cover of a trio of trash cans. A pistol cracked and flame streaked from its muzzle as the surviving goon opened fire at Clint. The Gunsmith heard a lead projectile whine against the iron framework of the balcony.

Clint held his revolver in both hands and aimed at the gunman's position. He opened fire. The thug was no doubt astonished when three .45 rounds rapidly punched into the flimsy metal trash cans he was using for cover. He couldn't have known he was trading lead with the Gunsmith or that Clint was armed with a specially modified weapon.

Clint Adams had altered his Colt to fire double-action. This meant he only had to pull the trigger due to the gun's self-cocking mechanism. He could thus fire more rapidly than a man armed with a single-action revolver.

An agonized scream from the alley informed Clint that one of his bullets had hit home. The enemy gunman suddenly burst from cover, his left arm dangling like a boneless rag. He still had his pistol, however, and snapped off a shot in Clint's direction.

The Gunsmith was far too battle-wise to remain in one position in a fire fight. He'd moved to the opposite end of the balcony. The would-be assassin's bullet didn't even come close. Glass shattered as it broke the windowpane.

Clint squeezed off another round. The hoodlum groaned and twisted in a hideous parody of a dance as another .45 slug crashed into his body. He stumbled several feet and made one last, feeble effort to use his pistol once more.

The Gunsmith's Colt snarled, pumping its last round squarely into the center of his opponent's chest. The impact of the heavy projectile kicked the man backward. He fell against a brick wall and slumped to the ground.

This time, he stayed down for good.

EIGHT

"Will you please explain how this happened, *Monsieur* Adams?" Lieutenant de Gasquet asked in a nasal monotone as he tapped his notepad with a pencil.

Clint Adams sighed as he approached the wiry little policeman. Lieutenant de Gasquet had met Clint after the Gunsmith took the battered old man to the hospital. The Gunsmith had intended to report the shooting to the police and to tell them about the old man, but he hadn't been prepared for a confrontation with someone like de Gasquet. The cop couldn't be as dumb as he acted, which meant he had to have a reason for asking Clint the same question four times.

He's probably not satisfied with my answers, the Gunsmith realized. *But what the hell else can I tell him except the truth?*

"Lieutenant," the Gunsmith began wearily, "I've already explained this. I was in my hotel room at the Royal House when I heard some commotion in the alley outside. Two men were beating up an elderly fella. It looked like they intended to kill him."

"So you shot and killed them both?" de Gasquet asked with a frown.

"I told them to stop," Clint explained once more. "They pulled guns and started shooting. I acted in self-defense."

37

"Are you accustomed to killing people and simply leaving their bodies to rot?" de Gasquet demanded. "This is New Orleans, not your wild West back in Texas."

"I noticed," Clint said dryly. "In Texas no one would question a man's right to shoot a couple fellas who were trying to kill you. Folks in Texas must be sort of simple because they seem to think the reason for defending your own life is obvious."

"Do you have any witnesses to this incident, *monsieur?*" the policeman asked. "Anyone who can support your story?"

"No." The Gunsmith shrugged. "But I'd hardly attack two total strangers and kill them in cold blood. What about the old man? You figure I beat him up and then brought him to the hospital? Come on, Lieutenant. You don't really believe that's what happened. Now, what sort of bullshit game are we playing?"

"Please, *Monsieur* Adams." De Gasquet held up his hands as if to fend off a physical attack. "Do try to calm yourself. I must question you about this business. Indeed, what you've told me is most certainly true."

"Yeah," Clint said dryly. "I know it's true. I was there."

"Of course." De Gasquet nodded. "And you acted in a very commendable manner, *monsieur*. You did not hesitate to come to the rescue of the old man who was being robbed by those two *cochons* . . . er, pigs, *oui?*"

"Robbed?" Clint blinked with surprise. "It sure didn't look like a robbery attempt to me. Those bastards really worked that old guy over. If they wanted his pocket money, they could have taken it without pounding the hell out of him."

"Who can understand the mind of the hoodlum?" De

Gasquet shrugged. "They are brutes who enjoy senseless violence—that is why we call them *apaches*."

"Well, I don't think they were trying to rob that poor old guy in the alley."

"But what other reason would they have to assault their victim?"

"I don't know," Clint admitted. "Shouldn't you try to find out?"

"The two hoodlums who attacked him are dead," de Gasquet said with a sigh. "I can not learn much from a corpse. It is thus doubtful that we shall ever know the answer."

"You can ask the old man when he recovers consciousness," the Gunsmith suggested.

"But you said yourself that he suffered a serious beating, *monsieur*," the cop replied. "He has certainly received a concussion. We would have to regard his version of the incident as a mere theory by an old man unable to think clearly."

Clint was getting irritated with de Gasquet's attitude. He decided it was time to rattle the policeman's cage.

"You don't seem very concerned about an attack on a New Orleans judge, Lieutenant," he said.

Lt. de Gasquet glared at Clint. "How did you know he is a judge?"

"I found a business card in his breast pocket," the Gunsmith replied. "It said our battered friend is Judge Henri Duboir."

"You are a very curious man, *Monsieur* Adams," de Gasquet remarked. "That could get you in trouble if you do not learn to control your inquisitive nature."

"So I've been told," Clint nodded. "What about the judge?"

"Actually, Henri Duboir is a retired judge."

"So you don't care if he gets his head kicked in?"

The policeman stiffened. "I have not said anything to deserve such an accusation from you, *monsieur*."

"It's what's you're *not* saying that bothers me, Lieutenant."

"I'll say one thing, Adams," de Gasquet began, his manner no longer polite and his voice hard and cold. "You'll do well not to pry into things that do not concern you. That can be a very dangerous habit—especially in New Orleans."

NINE

The Gunsmith was about to demand an explanation from the police lieutenant when a tall figure suddenly appeared at the end of the corridor and marched toward the pair. Clint was so surprised by the newcomer's flamboyant appearance he momentarily forgot about de Gasquet's remark.

The man strode purposefully toward them. He was tall, almost as tall as the Gunsmith, with a similarly long-limbed, lean body. He wore a dark blue suit with a red-lined cape draped over his shoulders. A brass-handled walking stick was clenched in his left fist.

"Marcel Duboir?" De Gasquet stared at the newcomer as if he'd encountered a ghost.

"Surprised to see me, eh, de Gasquet?" the man replied crisply. "That makes us even. I'm astonished that the New Orleans Department of Police would promote you to lieutenant. The Parish Commissioner must be getting a bit careless."

"I will ignore that remark because you are no doubt upset about what happened to your father, Marcel," the policeman replied coolly. "When did you return from Europe?"

"Don't change the subject," Marcel said sharply. "I just found out my father is in this hospital, the victim of a

41

vicious beating. Now, what can you add to that, de Gasquet?''

''Your father was attacked by a pair of *apaches,*'' the lieutenant replied. ''An attempted robbery.''

''The hell it was,'' Marcel stated bluntly. ''But of course, you don't have enough information to conduct an investigation, do you?''

''There is no need for that,'' de Gasquet told him. ''*Monsieur* Adams here shot and killed the *apaches* when he rescued your father. He brought the judge here to the hospital.''

Marcel turned to Clint and bowed. ''I am very grateful for what you've done, *monsieur*. I owe you my father's life. If there is anything I can do for you in return, you need only ask.''

''I didn't help your father because I wanted to be rewarded,'' the Gunsmith answered.

''I understand that, *monsieur*,'' Marcel assured him. ''A man of honor needs no reward for doing what is noble and just. His honor is part of his soul. He acts with courage and obeys his principles because he must. Your actions tonight were as natural for you as eating, drinking or getting an erection in the presence of a beautiful woman, *oui?*''

Clint smiled. ''Well, I don't know if I'd say it was quite *that* instinctive a reaction, but I didn't have to think about it. There wasn't much time to think. Those bastards were trying to beat the judge to death.''

''You do not know that, *monsieur*,'' de Gasquet cautioned.

''Did you get a chance to question the *apaches* before they died?'' Marcel asked Clint.

''No,'' the Gunsmith confessed. ''The only talking we

did was with lead. They were both dead before I climbed down the balcony ladder to the alley."

"Then you do not know why they attacked my father?"

"Sorry." Clint sighed. "All I can say is they were young men, muscular with hard faces. If we were in Texas or the Arizona Territory, I'd say they were probably former miners or railroad workers turned outlaw. For what it's worth, I don't think they were trying to rob your father either."

"The investigation of crimes is a matter for the police," de Gasquet declared. "You'll both do well to remember that."

"Leave it to the police," Marcel snorted. "You would ask me to trust you, de Gasquet? I'd sooner trust a fox to stand guard over a chicken coop."

"I've heard enough insults from you!" the policeman snapped. "Perhaps Adams is impressed by your melo-dramatic display of concern for your father, but I remem-ber you from before, Marcel. I was a patrolman when you were a boy. I saw you grow up from a worthless child to a worthless adult."

"Which you would certainly recognize since you see the face of such a person whenever you gaze into a mirror, *oui?*" Marcel replied.

"You are fortunate that dueling has been banned and I am an officer of the law," de Gasquet declared. "Other-wise I would confront you on the field of honor!"

"Oh?" Marcel smiled. "And who would you get to shoot me in the back?"

"You've always been good with words, Marcel," the cop stated. "But a sharp tongue never killed anyone—except occasionally the speaker himself."

"It's always nice to see old friends meet like this,"

Clint Adams commented dryly. "Maybe I should just let you two chat about things. . . ."

"Wait a moment, *s'il vous plaît*," Marcel urged. "At least allow me to buy you a drink, *Monsieur* Adams."

"Best offer I've heard all night," Clint agreed.

"Drink with him if you wish," de Gasquet told the Gunsmith. "But do not believe everything Marcel tells you. He has always been a rogue and an opportunist. If Judge Duboir could speak to us now, he would confirm this as well."

"The judge may have a few words for all three of you," a thickly built middle-aged man dressed in shirt-sleeves and a vest announced as he approached the trio. "Since he's still unconscious, I'll tell you what he'd probably say: 'Shut up and let me sleep.' This is a hospital, not a lecture hall. I'll thank you not to argue so in my hospital."

"Doctor," Marcel began, "how is my father? Will he be all right?"

"He has a broken arm and a couple cracked ribs," the doctor replied. "Some teeth were knocked out and his nose is broken, but otherwise he only suffered a lot of bruises. He's a tough fellow for a man his age. You'll be able to take him home tomorrow—providing you promise to make certain he rests. He'll need time to recover from that beating."

"Of course, Doctor," Marcel agreed. "I apologize for my behavior. *Monsieur* Adams and I are going to have a drink together, so we'll be leaving any minute now."

"What are we waiting for?" Clint inquired.

The sound of footsteps on the floor drew their attention to the end of the corridor. Two stocky, bearded figures strode toward them. Both men carried double-barrel shotguns and their expressions suggested they wouldn't hesitate to use their weapons if the need arose.

"Ah!" Marcel announced. "We do not have to wait for anything now. André and Phillippe are here."

"What are they doing with those shotguns?" the doctor demanded.

"Hopefully they will merely hold the guns for comfort during a long night's silent vigil," Marcel answered. "But just in case my father's enemies decide to again attempt to take his life while he lies helpless in a hospital bed, then André and Phillippe will welcome the assassins with buckshot and send them to Hell."

"*Zut!*" de Gasquet exclaimed. "Do you really think it is necessary to post guards at your father's door, Marcel?"

"It is necessary to protect my father, *oui*," the young Duboir declared. "And you can tell your friend Lacombe that the sheep will no longer be easy to shear and if he wants the wool he'll have to fight for it!"

TEN

Marcel Duboir escorted Clint Adams to a small tavern on Rue Deux. They ordered a bottle of wine and two glasses. Marcel paid for the drinks and they carried the bottle and goblets to a table.

"To a brave and honorable man," Marcel said, tapping his glass against Clint's.

"Right now I'm feeling more like a confused and curious man," the Gunsmith replied. "It's sort of like I walked into a theater right in the middle of a play."

"Are you sure you want to know any more about this business, *monsieur?*"

"Call me Clint," the Gunsmith said. "I had to kill two men tonight. They didn't leave me any other choice so I don't really wonder why, but I'd still like to know the reason they assaulted your father in the first place."

"Very well," the Frenchman agreed. "My father was a judge for almost twenty years here in New Orleans. He has always been a true believer and supporter of justice. Law and justice are not always the same, you know. He always did his very best to protect the innocent and punish the guilty. This has made him dearly loved by many people in the city."

"And it also got him some enemies?"

"Indeed," Marcel nodded. "And the Lacombe syndicate is the worst possible enemy to have in New Orleans.''

"Lacombe?" Clint began. "You mentioned that name at the hospital.''

"Gaston Lacombe," Marcel stated. "He owns a gambling house located near the waterfront and a riverboat which makes most of its profit as a floating casino.''

"Yeah," the Gunsmith remarked. "*La Reine Rouge*."

"That's right," Marcel said with surprise. "How did you know this?"

"Because I rode *La Reine Rouge* from Galveston," Clint explained. "I met Lacombe. In fact, he offered me a job.''

"A job?" Marcel stared at Clint.

"He wanted me to be one of his hired gunmen.''

"Your reputation as the Gunsmith must have appealed to him," Duboir mused.

Clint raised his eyebrows. "So you know about that?"

"*Oui*," Marcel smiled. "The West fascinates me. Someday, I hope to go there myself. It must be very exciting.''

"From time to time," Clint admitted.

"Naturally, I am familiar with the careers of such men as Wild Bill Hickok, Wyatt Earp and, of course, the Gunsmith.''

"Like I said, call me Clint," the Gunsmith told him. "I never wanted my reputation and I can't recall any time that it ever did anything but bring me trouble.''

"It is said you never start trouble, but you are superb at stopping it," Marcel remarked. "And you never work for evil men.''

"A couple times I've found myself on the wrong side," Clint confessed. "But I didn't stay there for long.''

"I know." Marcel nodded. "If Lacombe had been

more familar with your reputation, he would have known better than to ask you to join him.''

"Corrupt people always figure everybody else is as bad as they are,'' the Gunsmith said. "I also met Gaston's kid brother. The little bastard accused me of cheating at cards and pulled a gun on me.''

"That sounds like Roger Lacombe.'' Marcel frowned. "Bad-tempered young *cochon*. I don't suppose you were able to do the world a favor by killing him?''

"As a matter of fact, I saved his life.''

"I won't hold that against you.''

"Well, his attitude afterward convinced me to punch him in the mouth. Does that redeem me a bit?''

"A bit.'' Marcel smiled. "Anyway, the Lacombe gambling business is just the tip of the figurative iceberg. Lacombe is involved in white slavery, fencing stolen goods for other *apaches* in New Orleans and smuggling these ill-gotten goods to criminal traders at various ports along the Gulf of Mexico from here to Texas.''

"You seem well informed about Lacombe.''

"My father got most of this information. He's been gathering data about Lacombe's shady business ventures for years.''

"Why hasn't he gone to the police?''

"You saw the reason,'' Marcel answered. "Lieutenant de Gasquet is on Lacombe's payroll. He isn't the only policeman who's working for that bastard. We can't trust the police.''

"Something must have happened recently to make Lacombe take direct action against your father,'' Clint commented. "What was it?''

"Lacombe's newest enterprise,'' Marcel replied. "His syndicate has decided to force local shop owners and businessmen to pay protection 'insurance.' It's an idea that the Italian Black Hand has used for decades. The syndicate demands payment from a shopkeeper. If the man refuses, the *apaches* beat him up, wreck his place of business, burn down his house, whatever. Of course, they then warn the victim that the next time will be worse.''

"So they're paying Lacombe to be protected *from* Lacombe," Clint said.

"Exactly. And the locals are well aware of the syndicate's connections with the department of police, so they had nowhere to turn.''

"Until Judge Duboir decided to champion their cause.''

"Right again," Marcel replied. "My father declared war on the Lacombe syndicate. However, he's a judge and accustomed to fighting in courtrooms, not in the streets. The law is his weapon, and it has failed him. He has tried to organize the shopkeepers and businessmen to stand against Lacombe.''

"Stand against him as an organized fighting unit or as witnesses in a court?" Clint asked.

"The latter, naturally.'' Marcel sighed with exasperation. "Of course, the shop owners fear for their stores and their families. Father wants to sign petitions and have summons presented to Lacombe. He is not a man of violence, yet nothing less than violence will stop Lacombe.''

"Your views are quite different from your father's, Marcel.''

"*Oui*," the young man admitted. "What de Gasquet said is partly true. My father and I have had our differences in the past. He wanted me to study law, I wanted to be a poet. He thought I should get married, but I've always found the greatest pleasure about women to be their variety. None of that matters now. My father needs help and I will lay down my life to protect him if I must."

"A dead man can't help anyone, Marcel," the Gunsmith remarked. "It's better to lay down the enemies' lives than your own."

"Now that is a philosophy I can appreciate." Marcel smiled.

ELEVEN

Patches of fog had drifted into the city while Clint and Marcel conversed within the tavern. When they stepped outside, a blanket of gray mist had formed in the streets. The effect was eerie and sinister as strands of ghostly smoke curled and rolled with the breeze.

"The Royal House is almost two miles from here," Marcel remarked. "Shall we get a carriage?"

"Two miles isn't too far to walk." Clint shrugged.

"In New Orleans after dark it can be very far indeed," Marcel warned. "Gangs lurk in the alleys, and even youngsters, some barely teenagers, have formed small gangs which specialize on preying on lone pedestrians. They are like packs of wild dogs, these hoodlums."

"Where are you staying, Marcel?"

"In my father's house," the young Duboir replied. "It is perhaps six blocks from here."

"A long way to travel by foot in the dangerous streets of New Orleans." Clint laughed.

"It does not frighten me, my friend," Marcel said. "But I do not take it lightly."

"Okay," the Gunsmith began. "I'll meet you at the hospital tomorrow morning. We'll take the judge home and talk to him about this Lacombe business."

"This isn't your fight, Clint—"

"I didn't say I was going to get directly involved," the Gunsmith declared. "But I might be able to give you fellas some advice and—"

His sentence died abruptly when he spotted two figures out of the corner of his eye. Two men armed with clubs were rushing forward, about to attack Clint and Marcel. Three more assailants suddenly appeared from the opposite direction. It was a simple two-prong attack ambush with Clint and his friend right in the middle—the worst possible position to be in when confronted by multiple opponents.

"*Merde!*" Marcel exclaimed as he raised his cane to block a cudgel swing.

Clint concentrated on the first two. He prepared to reach for his Colt .45, but the assailants were already on top of him. The Gunsmith dodged a slashing club attack and rammed his right fist into the hoodlum's stomach.

The thug groaned. Clint drove a left hook into the man's kidney and followed up with an upper cut under his ribcage. With a gagging gasp, the hood doubled up. Clint raised his arms high, clasped his hands together and chopped them into the nape of his opponent's neck as hard as he could. The blow could have been fatal, but the Gunsmith wasn't concerned about the physical welfare of a man who had tried to bash his brains in.

As Clint's first opponent fell to the fog-laced ground another *apache* charged forward and swung his cudgel at Clint's head. The Gunsmith stepped forward and grabbed the man's arm behind the club. He pivoted sharply and yanked his opponent's armpit into his shoulder.

The Gunsmith bent swiftly and executed a Flying Mare which sent the startled man hurtling over his back. The hoodlum sailed six feet and crashed to the cobblestones.

He lay stunned in the street. Clint spied a discarded cudgel at his feet and quickly picked it up.

He glanced over at Marcel Duboir to see the young Frenchman was holding his own against another pair. Marcel's right leg swung a high roundhouse kick which knocked a bowie knife out of an assailant's grasp. Duboir pivoted with the motion of his kick and rapidly stabbed the end of his cane into his opponent's gut. The man doubled up and Marcel whipped a knee into his attacker's face.

As the thug fell to the ground, his partner attacked Marcel from behind. Clint prepared to go to his friend's assistance, but Marcel didn't need any help. His left leg kicked backward like a mule, driving his heel into the attacker's midsection. Before the dazed *apache* could recover from the blow, Marcel spun and launched a high side-kick. The bottom of his shoe crashed into the point of his opponent's jaw. The hood's feet left the ground and he landed heavily on his back.

The Gunsmith turned to face the fifth and last aggressor. The scrawny, rat-faced man would have seemed an easy opponent if he hadn't held a long-bladed dagger in his fist. Clint had encountered knife artists before and he could tell this one was an expert with cold steel. He held the knife low, in an underhand grip, ideal for thrusts and slashes aimed at the abdomen or ribs.

Clint decided to act first, planning to feint a swing to the man's head and then quickly chop the club across the *apache's* wrist to disarm him. The guy was too small and skinny to present much of a threat without a dagger . . . or so Clint assumed.

Suddenly, the scrawny hoodlum jumped high into the air like a jackrabbit. His behavior startled and baffled the Gunsmith. Then Clint glimpsed a hobnail boot which hurtled at his face. He jerked his head aside. The kick caught him on the left cheekbone.

The Gunsmith lost his balance and fell to the street. Dots of light popped inside his head and his vision blurred for a second or two. He blinked twice and looked up to see the skinny shadow fleeing down the street.

"Clint?" Marcel's voice said urgently. "Are you alright, *mon ami?*"

"Yeah," the Gunsmith muttered as Marcel helped him to his feet. "I just never fought a fella who thought he was a kangaroo before."

"*Savate,*" Marcel explained. "It is a French form of foot-boxing. Some of these *apaches* are familiar with it. Something to bear in mind if you ever get into a brawl with them again, *oui?*"

"Uh-huh," Clint agreed, gingerly placing his fingers at the bruise on his cheek. The thug had kicked him in the center of his scar. "From the way you handled yourself, you're more than slightly familiar with *savate* yourself."

Marcel smiled. "I've learned a few techniques over the years. But do not feel badly, you defeated two *apaches* as well. Of course, I did not get kicked in the face. . . ."

"You sure know how to cheer a fella up, Marcel," the Gunsmith said sourly. "You figure these guys were acting on Lacombe's orders?"

"Probably," Duboir replied. "It could have been an attempted robbery, but I doubt it."

"That's what I figure too," Clint agreed.

One of the *apaches* groaned as he began to regain consciousness. Clint had had enough exercise for one night. He drew his pistol and aimed it at the thug's face. Marcel kicked the man in the ribs.

"Who sent you?" the Gunsmith demanded, cocking his revolver to accent his demand.

The man stared up at him fearfully, but did not speak. Marcel snapped an angry sentence in rapid French. The *apache* replied in the same language.

"He says he and his comrades were paid five dollars each to attack us," Marcel told Clint. "They did not know the man who hired them nor did they ask his name. He merely told them he'd be watching and he'd pay them another five dollars after they took care of us."

"Just how were they supposed to take care of us?" the Gunsmith asked.

"Fatally," Marcel replied. "It would appear Lacombe is prepared to take this war to its ultimate conclusion."

"Kill or be killed." *Some vacation*, Clint thought.

TWELVE

Henri Duboir was released from the hospital the following morning. Clint and Marcel were waiting for the judge with a hansom cab. Henri climbed into the carriage and they rode to the judge's home on Rue Croissant.

Clint hadn't had an opportunity to examine Henri's face and gestures in detail. On the night of the assault, he'd been too busy trying to save the old man's life to notice such things. Henri was not as old as his gray hair suggested. Clint guessed the man was only about ten years his senior. Still, a man in his fifties was considered well past his prime—something that the Gunsmith tried not to think about as each birthday came up.

Although older and heavier than his son, Henri and Marcel still bore a family resemblance. They had the same hazel eyes and strong lantern jaw. Henri's nose may have been as long and straight as Marcel's if it hadn't been broken with a bandage taped across the bridge.

"I am told you came to my rescue, *monsieur*," Henri said through swollen lips. "I thank you more than words can say and I commend you on your marksmanship. I understand you killed the two men who attacked me, *oui?*"

"They called it," Clint replied. "And lost."

"I believe in capital punishment." Henri shrugged. "And I can't say I'm sorry those two are dead."

"Nobody's exactly ready to have a wake in their honor," the Gunsmith remarked. "But unfortunately there are lots of fellas available to replace them."

Henri turned to Marcel. "How much does he know?"

"Everything," the younger man replied. "Considering what's happened, he had a right to know all the details."

"We will discuss this when we get home," Henri said, glancing suspiciously at the carriage driver. "Where there are not so many ears to hear us."

They rode in silence the rest of the way to the judge's house. Clint had expected a grand mansion, but the dwelling proved to be a handsome brownstone, considerably smaller than he would have guessed. A well-cared-for rose garden and trimmed lawn surrounded the house. Ornate, yet practical iron bars were mounted in the windows.

After they entered the house, Henri suggested they go to the parlor. Marcel helped his father into the cozy sitting room. Henri asked to be placed on the large sofa.

"Please help yourselves to the liquor cabinet," he urged.

"It's a little early for me," Clint replied.

"*Oui,*" Marcel agreed. "I think I'll pass as well."

"As you like," Henri nodded. "But I'd like a glass of brandy. Marcel, *s'il vous plaît?*"

"Of course, Father," the younger man answered as he headed for the liquor cabinet.

"Now, *Monsieur* Adams . . ." Henri began.

"Clint," the Gunsmith corrected.

"Friends should be on first-name terms," Henri agreed. "And as a friend, I must warn you that you've already gotten involved in our war with the Lacombe syndicate and to continue to associate with us could prove to be very dangerous."

"Your son and I were *both* attacked last night, Henri," Clint remarked. "That sort of puts me in the middle whether I want to be or not."

"You could leave New Orleans," Henri suggested.

"I came all the way from Texas." The Gunsmith grinned. "You expect me to leave already?"

"Clint and I discussed this matter last night," Marcel explained as he carried a balloon glass of brandy to his father. "He's decided to help us."

"And I agree with Marcel," Clint added. "We'll have to fight Lacombe with force, not words and paper."

"Do you know what you're saying?" Henri asked. "You're suggesting shopkeepers, businessmen and fishermen do battle with Lacombe's killers. They're no match for *apaches* to whom violence is a way of life."

"A while back," Clint began, "I was in Mexico looking for an American girl who'd been kidnapped by a *bandido* known as *el Espectro*. A village of *peones* fought the bandit's gang. Those peasants weren't accustomed to violence either—except as victims of it—yet they defeated the *bandidos*."

"With your help, eh, Clint!" Marcel inquired.

"Yeah," the Gunsmith admitted. "But I was only one more man. The *peones* had decided to get up off their knees and fight. That's why they won."

"I'm afraid I can't believe that being morally right is enough to guarantee a victory." Henri frowned.

"Of course it isn't," Clint agreed. "You also need a good, practical plan of action. Don't forget, we'll have one big plus in our favor."

"Really?" Henri raised his eyebrows. "I can't think of what that might be."

"Lacombe's people aren't expecting us to hit back," the Gunsmith explained. "They're used to doing pretty much as they please without having to worry about any-body shooting their heads off.''

"That's not such a great advantage," Henri insisted. "Considering the fact Lacombe's *apaches* are far more inclined to commit such acts of violence than the people I'm trying to help."

"Hell," Clint muttered. "Your people want to keep their businesses, right? They want to protect their families from Lacombe. How do they intend to do that? By con-tinuing to pay blackmail to the very man they're afraid of?"

"I don't think they want their neighborhoods turned into battlefields either," Henri replied dryly. "They came to me to try to prevent violence, not encourage it."

"They want to be safe." Marcel snorted. "They're afraid of Lacombe, Clint. You've already seen why. He didn't waste any time sending a goon squad after us, did he?"

"And we fought them and won," the Gunsmith said. "If those good people want to be safe, tell them to dig a big ditch and cover themselves up with dirt. Risk is part of life. Only the dead are safe."

"That isn't very reassuring." Henri sighed.

"Neither is the idea of having to fight Lacombe's syndicate without anybody to back our play," Clint told him. "If your people aren't willing to fight for their own sake, don't ask me to lay my life on the line for them."

"Oh, they'll fight," Marcel assured Clint. "André and Phillippe eagerly volunteered to guard my father. Plenty of others wanted to go too."

"But lots of others are still too scared, right?" Clint inquired.

"We'll talk to them." Henri sighed. "I'm afraid you're right, Clint. Perhaps the only way to deal with violence is by resorting to more violence.''

"From what you've told me, I'd say there isn't any other choice in this case,'' the Gunsmith replied.

"We're very grateful for your involvement in this matter, Clint,'' Henri began. "But why are you doing this? After all, this isn't your fight.''

"You were a judge, Henri.'' Clint shrugged. "I'd figure you'd understand.''

Henri Duboir raised his eyebrows. "How's that?''

"Injustice should be every man's battle,'' the Gunsmith answered. "And now that I've shared my idealistic motto, we'd better figure out what the hell we're going to do next.''

THIRTEEN

The desk clerk recognized Clint Adams when the Gunsmith entered the lobby of the Royal House. He greeted Clint with a nervous nod. The Gunsmith returned the gesture, well aware the clerk was less than pleased to see him. Clint couldn't blame the man. After all, good hotel guests don't get into gunfights within less than an hour after checking into a room.

"Good afternoon, sir," the clerk said, a tremble in his voice.

"God, I hope so." Clint grinned.

The clerk didn't respond to the joke.

"Well." The Gunsmith sighed. "I hope you won't be too disappointed, but I've decided to check out of the Royal House a few days early."

"Oh." The clerk blinked with surprise. "Well, if that is what you want to do . . ."

"I'm about to head up to my room to get my gear, friend," Clint answered.

"The hotel owes you some money, sir," the clerk stated. "I'll get it for you."

"Fine," the Gunsmith agreed as he moved toward the stairs. "I'll pick it up when I come down."

"Sir?" the clerk began urgently. He bit his lip before he continued. "There are some visitors waiting for you in your room, sir."

"Visitors?" Clint asked sharply. "You let them into my quarters while I was gone?"

"I had to, sir. . . ." the clerk began lamely.

"How many of them are up there?"

"Three," the man replied. "But they promised me no one would be hurt. . . ."

"And I'm sure they looked like men of honor." Clint clucked his tongue with disgust.

"I'm—I'm sorry, sir."

"Hell." The Gunsmith sighed. "At least you warned me about them. Thanks for doing that much."

Clint cautiously mounted the stairs, his right hand resting on the grips of his holstered .45 Colt revolver. He wondered if the Lacombe syndicate could actually be bold enough to have him murdered in broad daylight in a public place.

He mentally pictured the corridor above and considered what methods he might use if he wanted to ambush someone. There wasn't much cover in the hallway. Clint remembered a window at the end of the corridor, but he hadn't checked to see if it had a balcony. A man could be stationed there. The others would probably be waiting for him in his room or possibly positioned in other rooms, ready to attack when he reached his door.

Why make themselves so obvious? Clint wondered. He'd survived numerous ambushes, including several in hotel rooms. More than once, a sniper had fired at him from a distance. On one occasion, he had found a rattlesnake in his bed. Certainly the Lacombes would have realized that a rifleman on a rooftop could pick Clint off with a well placed bullet through the window. That would be less risky than sending three men up to his room.

Clint decided this could only mean one of three things. First, whoever his visitors were, they weren't part of the

Lacombe syndicate. If this proved to be the case, then the three men were probably police or friends of the Duboirs. The latter seemed unlikely because Marcel and Henri hadn't mentioned that they intended to send anyone.

Another possibility was that Lacombe had sent someone to try to talk Clint out of helping the Duboirs and they didn't plan to do any shooting . . . at least, not yet. The third possibility worried Clint the most. Lacombe may have decided to show everyone just how invulnerable to the law he really was. What better way than to openly murder the Gunsmith in broad daylight, heedless of witnesses or the police? Such a public execution would terrify the people Lacombe was blackmailing.

The idea didn't make Clint feel very good either.

Well, Clint thought, *I'll find out in a second . . . one way or the other.*

He reached the head of the stairs. A hard-faced figure dressed in a blue suit stood in the corridor. Clint had previously seen the man on *La Reine Rouge*. He was the steward named Debray.

"You look different out of uniform," the Gunsmith remarked.

"*Monsieur* Lacombe wishes to talk with you," Debray told him in a flat, emotionless voice.

"If he thinks I'm going to give you my gun, he's nuts," Clint stated.

"I received no such orders, *monsieur*," Debray shrugged. He gestured at Clint's room. "Please, my employer is waiting for you."

"Move away from the door and keep your hands where I can see them," Clint instructed.

Debray sighed as he stepped backward and raised his hands. "If we wanted you dead," he commented, "you would already be a corpse, *monsieur*."

"Humor me," the Gunsmith replied, although he knew Debray was probably right.

Clint approached the door carefully. It was unlocked and slightly ajar. He stood clear of the door and nudged it open with the toe of his boot, half expecting a gunshot in reply.

"No one will harm you, Clint," a voice declared from within the room. "Please, come in. I am a busy man and I want to make this conversation brief and to the point."

Slowly, the Gunsmith peeked around the corner to see Gaston Lacombe seated on the loveseat inside. The kingpin's burly bodyguard, Jules, stood by the bed. The big man's arms were folded on his massive chest, his sawed-off shotgun propped against a wall close by.

"How's the casino business, Gaston?" Clint inquired as he stepped across the threshold.

"My business always does well," Lacombe replied.

The Gunsmith suddenly slammed a boot into the door, kicking it hard enough to smack it into the wall. Lacombe chuckled.

"No, Clint," he said. "There is no hidden assassin lurking behind the door. Nor is there one beneath your bed or waiting outside on the balcony. Give me some credit for intelligence, *mon ami*. Surely you do not think *I* would be here if I intended to have you murdered."

"That's a good point, Lacombe," Clint admitted as he entered the room. "Men like you never handle your own dirty work."

"So we are no longer on first name terms, eh?" Gaston asked, lighting a cigar.

"Be kind of silly under the circumstances, don't you think?"

"*Comme vous voulez.*" Gaston shrugged. "I'm certain you know why I am here, *oui?*"

"I've got a suspicion or two about your reason," the Gunsmith replied. "Why don't you tell me so I'll know for sure?"

"Last night you came to the rescue of a retired judge named Duboir."

"And you wanted to commend me for being a good Samaritan?" Clint asked with a straight face.

"How droll," Gaston replied. "Since you spent the morning at the Duboirs' house, I'm certain the judge and his emotional son Marcel told you a lot of absurd stories about me."

"How did you know where I was this morning?" the Gunsmith asked.

"*Nothing* happens in New Orleans that I'm not aware of," Gaston declared.

"Jesus," Clint muttered. "You could write a hell of a gossip column in the newspaper, couldn't you?"

"Answer *Monsieur* Lacombe," Jules growled, his voice deep and thickly accented.

"Tell your watchdog that he might be big, but a .45 bullet between the eyes will cut him down to a lifeless dwarf pronto," Clint told Gaston, but his eyes were trained on Jules.

"Jules will not harm you unless I tell him to," Gaston assured Clint. "However, I advise you not to insult either Jules or myself. A couple of years ago, a man pulled a gun on Jules and shot him three times. Jules absorbed the bullets and killed his opponent. After the slugs were removed, Jules rested for two days and returned to work. As you can see, he's as healthy as a young bull."

"And just as smart," Clint remarked. "Okay, Lacombe. I admit that Henri, Marcel and I mentioned you in our conversation. Is that a crime in New Orleans?"

"That depends on what you said about me," Gaston

replied. He didn't seem to be joking.

"You know so goddamn much, you tell me." Clint shrugged.

"*Anglo bâtard!*" Jules hissed. He unfolded his arms and stepped forward.

"*Pas encore*, Jules," Gaston ordered. The man stopped, stepped backward and placed his arms on his chest once more.

"Nice training," Clint mused. "Does he roll over and fetch as well?"

"Don't tempt your good fortune, Adams," Gaston warned. "You're an intelligent man. You should realize when a risk is foolish. Evoking my anger isn't wise, I assure you."

"What the Duboirs and I discussed is private, Lacombe," Clint told him.

"Very well." Gaston sighed. "You saved my brother from that card cheat on board *La Reine Rouge*, so I'll give you some good advice."

"I'm listening."

"This matter between the Duboirs and myself does not concern you. Stay out of it."

"I take it kind of personal when a gang of hired coyotes on two legs attack me," Clint stated.

"Of course I know nothing of that." Gaston shrugged. "But I suspect that the gang had been ordered to attack Marcel. You had simply made the mistake of being in his company at the time."

"Seems to me it was the *apaches* who made the mistake, Lacombe."

"They were armed with clubs and knives," the Frenchman remarked. "Next time, they might carry guns."

"And they'd better know how to use them," Clint said in a flat hard voice.

"*Incroyable!*" Gaston declared, throwing his hands up in the air. "I offered you a job which would have paid quite well and required no genuine risk to your life and limb, and you refused. Yet you are now joining forces with a troublesome old man and his playboy son. I'm certain they can not pay you as well as I, if indeed they have offered you any money at all."

"Reckon I'm just a bit odd about the company I keep, Lacombe," the Gunsmith told him.

"Oh, one has quite a bit of company in a graveyard, Adams." Gaston sighed as he rose from the loveseat. "I believe our conversation is over. However, Jules will now assist me in delivering a small edification for your sake."

"Edification?" Clint asked, turning to face the huge bodyguard, his hand ready to draw the Colt from leather.

"A lesson, so to speak," Gaston explained. "Don't worry. You won't need your gun. Jules!"

The big man nodded in response. He then stepped forward, limping slightly as he approached the small wooden desk in the Gunsmith's room. Jules suddenly snarled and lashed out with his right foot.

The desk exploded. Jules's kick splintered the wooden top and caused the frame to collapse. He swept his foot into the wreckage and sent it hurtling across the room to smash against the wall. The remains of the desk resembled a pile of kindling.

Clint stared at Jules in disbelief. He had previously thought the giant dragged his foot because his leg was lame. However, if Jules qualified as a cripple, the term "helpless" certainly didn't apply in his case.

"*Aaiiee!*" Jules bellowed as he turned to deliver a hard

side-kick to the chest of drawers.

The face of the chest was caved in by the powerful blow. Two drawers were cracked and the bearing rail between them was splintered. Jules swung his leg once more, chopping the edge of his foot into the side panel of the bureau. Wood shattered and the furniture tipped over and crashed to the floor in a ruined heap.

"The maid service isn't going to like you guys," Clint commented, trying to conceal his astonishment with the remark.

"I've already paid for the damages, Adams," Gaston assured him. "I trust this lesson is not beyond your understanding?"

"If I've got good furniture, I shouldn't invite Jules over to see it?"

"I'm not amused, Adams," Gaston said sternly. "If you get in my way, I can have you crushed"—he tilted his head at the splintered chest of drawers—"like that."

With that, Gaston Lacombe marched from the room. Jules sneered at Clint and limped after his master like an obedient dog. He stopped to seize the doorknob.

"Hey, Jules," Clint began, "didn't your mama ever tell you to clean up a mess after you've made it?"

The big man's face contorted with anger. He slammed the door shut hard.

"I guess not." The Gunsmith shrugged.

FOURTEEN

None of the Gunsmith's belongings were missing. This didn't surprise him. Gaston Lacombe may have been many things which were less than honorable, but no one could call him a petty thief.

Of course, Clint realized, Gaston and his men had certainly had ample time to inspect the Gunsmith's weaponry which he'd left in the room. However, the only gun Clint had left in plain view had been his Springfield .45 caliber carbine. He checked the saddle gun and discovered it was still loaded. Clint worked the lever and cocked back the hammer. Both worked fine.

Then he gazed into the receiver. A cold smile crept across the Gunsmith's lips. The firing pin had been removed. *Nice try, you bastards*, he thought. He made a mental note to stop at a gunshop and purchase a replacement for the missing part.

He opened his saddlebags and checked the gear in them. Nothing was missing, but he was sure the intruders had gone through the bags. That wouldn't matter much. The boxes of .45 ammunition were still there and Lacombe wouldn't have had time to tamper with the shells. *But he could have replaced the boxes with cartridges that had the primers removed*, Clint thought. He decided he'd better buy some fresh shells just to be safe.

A lone box of .22-caliber ammo was also in the bag.

Gaston might realize that this meant Clint could have a small hideout gun. This, in fact, was the case. The Gunsmith frequently carried a diminutive New Line Colt pistol in his belt under his shirt. Lacombe hadn't found the gun because Clint was carrying it. After the run-in with the *apache* gang, he'd decided to take the belly gun with him that morning.

The Gunsmith gathered up his belongings and left his room. The desk clerk sheepishly handed Clint his refund and muttered an apology. Clint ignored him, took the money and left the hotel. He headed straight for the livery stable and led Duke from his stall. To his relief, the horse had not been harmed by Lacombe's goons. Perhaps Gaston hadn't known which animal belonged to Clint. Then again, he'd tried to frighten the Gunsmith into retreating from his involvement with the Duboirs. Maybe he'd wanted Clint to have a horse so he could leave New Orleans immediately if the scare tactic worked.

Clint made one stop when he located a gunshop. He purchased the firing pin for his Springfield and two boxes of 240-grain, .45-caliber cartridges. Then he rode on to Judge Duboir's home on Rue Croissant.

Marcel Duboir and the two muscular bodyguards, André and Phillippe, met Clint at the gate. Clint noticed the bearded shopkeepers still carried their shotguns and appeared ready to use the weapons if the need popped up. *Good*, he thought. *Now if we can just get enough of our other allies to adopt the same attitude.*

"Ah, Clint!" Marcel greeted, waving his cane at the Gunsmith. "I'm glad you've returned so early. Do you still want to do a little reconnaissance today?"

"Yeah," Clint replied as he swung down from Duke's back. "It never hurts to know as much as possible about an enemy's headquarters."

"I agree," Marcel said. "But we'll have to be careful if we're going to spy on Lacombe's waterfront lair."

"Don't I know it." The Gunsmith nodded. "Gaston and a couple of his hootowls were waiting for me at the hotel."

Marcel raised his eyebrows. *"Merde alors!"*

"What the hell does *merde* mean?" the Gunsmith wondered.

"Shit," Marcel translated. "But *merde* certainly sounds better, doesn't it?"

"So does the Spanish word *mierda*," Clint added. "In English, 'shit' just sounds like shit."

"We can discuss linguistics later, *mon ami*," Marcel urged. "What happened at the hotel?"

"Not much really," Clint shrugged. "Lacombe tried to talk me out of helping you folks. He made a few threats and a big bastard called Jules kicked the hell out of my furniture. I mean that literally. You wouldn't believe the way he busted up a desk and a chest of drawers with just a couple kicks."

"Oh, I believe you," Marcel assured him. "Jules is a very dangerous fellow. He was formerly a stevedore on the docks, feared and respected even by the others of his kind . . . and stevedores are very tough men and not impressed easily. Jules was also very skilled in *savate*, but unfortunately he was a terrible bully and used this ability for evil purposes. They say he was even then in the employ of an *apache* gang and used to earn pocket money by assaulting victims for the hoodlums."

"But he drags his right foot as if he's lame, yet he used it to kick my furniture into matchsticks."

"But of course," Marcel replied. "You see, Jules crossed the wrong person or persons a few years ago. Someone, probably a *lot* of *someones*, gave him a severe beating and chopped off his right foot at the ankle with an axe. Some say he was punished in this manner because he kicked an *apache* chief in the *testicules*. Whatever, one thing is certain: Jules was fitted with an artificial foot made of steel and leather. I've heard it can be a fearsome weapon.''

"You heard right," Clint confirmed. "He kicks like he's got a sledgehammer for a foot."

"He *does*," Marcel declared. "And don't forget he is trained in *savate* as well. That makes him extremely dangerous indeed."

"Well," Clint mused, "a steel foot and French kick-boxing still isn't a match for this." He patted the Colt .45 on his hip.

"Quite true," Marcel agreed. "At least, I hope so. At any rate, why don't you take this beautiful horse around back to the stables and we'll be on our way?"

"How are we going to travel?" Clint inquired. "Lacombe has been able to keep track of us pretty well so far. He's got somebody watching this house too."

"We'll walk from here to a nice little place I know." Marcel smiled. "You'll enjoy it. I assure you."

"What sort of place?"

"A restaurant," Marcel replied. "Among other things."

"Okay, I haven't had lunch yet," the Gunsmith commented dryly. "But do you think we should waste time eating in a restaurant?"

"A visit to *Le Café d'Amour* is never a waste of time," Marcel insisted with a sly grin. "You'll see."

FIFTEEN

The Gunsmith and Marcel Duboir strolled along Rue Delié. Clint occasionally glanced over his shoulder, half-expecting to see a gang of Lacombe's *apaches* stalking them. Naturally, there were other people walking the streets of New Orleans that day, but none of them seemed to be paying special attention to Clint and Marcel.

This didn't give the Gunsmith any cause for comfort. Lacombe's syndicate had kept track of Clint's activities since he'd gotten involved with the Duboirs. They were certainly following the pair at that moment. The fact Clint hadn't noticed a tail merely meant whoever shadowed them was damn good at it. Intelligent opponents worried the Gunsmith more than musclebound brutes or gunhawks. With his .45 on his hip, Clint was a match for any man in a face-to-face confrontation. Lacombe was too smart to use such heavy-handed methods against the Gunsmith. Clint could only guess what the cunning gangster would conjure up as a means of dealing with him.

Although Marcel also realized that the Lacombe syndicate was a monstrous, powerful organization capable of tracking their every move and striking at any moment, the young Frenchman didn't seem the least bit concerned about the matter. He strolled along the sidewalk, his walking stick tapping the pavement in rhythm with his long-legged stride. Clint was apprehensive about Marcel's cavalier attitude. Yet he recalled how Duboir had handled himself in the fight against the *apache* gang. Marcel was far more formidable than he appeared. Still, a brawl with club-wielding opponents and a gunfight are very different types of battles. How well would Marcel do if the enemy started throwing lead at them?

Suddenly, something occurred to the Gunsmith. He had not noticed a bulge under Marcel's armpit or at his hip that would suggest his friend carried a gun.

"Hey, Marcel," he asked. "What sort of pistol do you favor?"

"Oh, a .44 caliber percussion pistol," the Frenchman replied.

"Cap and ball revolver?"

"Single-shot dueling pistol."

"Great," Clint muttered sourly. "We might find ourselves in the middle of a shooting gallery with us as the targets, and you're carrying a one-shot muzzle-loader!"

"No." Marcel shrugged. "I don't have a gun with me right now."

"Shit," the Gunsmith groaned. "What do you intend to do if Lacombe's hoods start shooting at us? Figure you can kick the bullets out of the air with that fancy *savate* stuff?"

"Is it not foolish to carry a weapon if you aren't familiar with its use?" Marcel asked. "In New Orleans, a gentleman learns how to handle a sword and a dueling pistol in case he needs to use them on the field of honor. He does not learn how to use a revolver because we do not quickdraw here, *oui?*"

"I thought duels had been banned in this city."

"Officially, yes." Marcel nodded. "But traditions do not end simply because legislation stands in their way. It is more important to obey the demands of one's honor than any local law.''

"It is also important to stay alive," Clint declared. "Lacombe isn't going to fight us in a formal duel, Marcel. You can't expect him to appreciate your fine sense of honor.''

"No," the other man admitted. "But you are the Gunsmith. Certainly your ability with a gun will compensate for my lack of skill.''

"Jesus," Clint whispered, rolling his eyes with exasperation.

At last, they reached *Le Café d'Amour*. It was a sidewalk café, modeled on the famous dining establishments of Paris. Canopies on stalks jutted from the centers of circular tabletops. Three stunning beauties waited on the customers.

"Traditionally," Marcel explained, "a sidewalk café only employs waiters, however, no one seems to mind this particular variation.''

"Some traditions can be overlooked," Clint agreed.

The three waitresses were lovely. One girl was a tall, sleek brunette with alabaster skin. Another had clipped blond hair and a full figure with large breasts and wide hips. Last, but not least, was a short, slender girl with long raven-black hair and an olive complexion. Her dark brown eyes were enormous and a wide smile revealed sparkling white teeth, a stunning contrast to her dark skin.

"I told you." Marcel smiled. "You'll enjoy this place, *oui?*''

"Sure looks nice," Clint agreed, watching the girls' rear ends gyrate as they moved from table to table.

The blonde spotted Marcel. *"Gut Gott!"* she exclaimed. "It ist our best customer, *Herr* Duboir!"

"Jawol, Greta," Marcel replied. *"Ich bin es!"*

"So I see." She approached the Frenchman and embraced his waist. "And where did you learn to speak *deutsch* so badly?"

"I spent a year and a half in Europe," Marcel said as he kissed her cheek. "I'm afraid I didn't learn much German while I was there."

"Just enough to romance the girls, eh?" Greta laughed.

The other two girls joined them. All three women looked at Clint with appreciation. The brunette spoke her mind.

"Who is your handsome friend, Marcel?" she asked.

"Clint Adams," the Frenchman replied. "Clint, meet Greta, Jeanette and Susie."

"A pleasure to meet you all," the Gunsmith nodded.

"Welcome to *Le Café d'Amour*," Jeanette, the brunette, said. "You will have lunch, *oui*? May I suggest *la côtelette d'agneau*?"

"It sounds almost as delicious as your lips, *ma cherie*," Marcel agreed. "Where shall we sit? Please, do not fight over us, eh, ladies?"

"I have a table available," the dark-eyed Susie declared. "It will be my pleasure to service you."

Clint glanced at her wide moist lips and wondered if her remark referred to more than food. Susie led the Gunsmith and Marcel to a table and asked what sort of wine they'd like with the meal.

"A *rosé* will do nicely," Marcel answered. "Not too sweet, but with good body and a bit dry. How does that sound to you, Clint?"

"Fine," the Gunsmith agreed, not wishing to admit he didn't know what the hell they were talking about.

"I will bring you your meals immediately," Susie promised. *"Bon appétit."*

Clint watched the girl hurry away to the kitchen. "You seem pretty popular around here," he remarked.

"*Oui*," Marcel confessed with a trace of pride in his tone. "These girls are all friends with one another. Such good friends, in fact, that they do not mind sharing in all things. I have made love to all three of them many times, yet they are not envious of one another. It is a perfect relationship, is it not?"

"Couldn't be much better," the Gunsmith agreed. He was quite a lady's man himself, yet he couldn't top Marcel on that score. However, he didn't envy Marcel. Eventually someone would get hurt if the sexual playground continued.

"These girls enjoy sex, *mon ami*," Marcel told him. "When this business with Lacombe is over, we must return here. You should not leave New Orleans until you have sampled all three of these wonderful love goddesses."

"Let's take care of Lacombe first," the Gunsmith advised.

"But of course." Marcel grinned. "For now, let us enjoy our dinner. It may be our last meal, *oui?*"

"I suppose Lacombe's headquarters will still be waiting for us later." Clint sighed.

"Indeed," Marcel agreed. "Now, let us see about our transportation. Greta?"

The blond waitress hurried to their table. "*Ja*, my dearest?"

"Do you still have that buckboard, *ma cherie?*"

"The wagon belongs to my brother," Greta answered. "But, *ja*, he still has it."

"Fine," Marcel replied. "Would he be willing to let us borrow the wagon for a while?"

"We won't borrow it really," Clint corrected. "We'll

rent it. Say, twenty dollars for its use for the rest of the day?''

''Twenty dollars?'' Greta asked in astonishment. ''What are you up to, Marcel? You've never done anything really criminal. You haven't decided to rob a bank or something, have you?''

''Of course not,'' he assured her. ''We need a wagon and we're willing to pay for it. I can't tell you more.''

''We'll return your brother's rig in the morning,'' Clint promised. ''If it is damaged, we'll pay for the entire wagon.''

''You're in trouble, aren't you, Marcel?''

''I'm involved in something you don't want to know about,'' the Frenchman stated. ''Please, Greta. We need that wagon.''

''I'll talk to Heinz.'' She sighed.

''Now?'' Marcel urged.

''*Ja*,'' Greta nodded wearily. ''When do you need the wagon?''

''Try to have it ready for us by the time we finish our meal. Don't bring it here. Have Heinz leave the buckboard in the alley between the restaurant and the public urinal.''

''Is somebody watching you, Marcel?'' Greta asked.

''Probably,'' he admitted.

''But don't look around,'' Clint warned her. ''Don't do anything to attract attention to yourself when you leave.''

''*Gott in Himmel!*'' the girl rasped. ''One of these days you're going to get into such trouble no one will be able to help you, Marcel.''

''I'll reform and become a very docile fellow after this is over.'' He grinned. ''I may even get married and raise a family.''

''If you must lie,'' Greta began, ''at least make it believable.''

Marcel laughed. "You know me too well, *ma cherie*. Will you also ask Heinz to include a couple of rain slickers and perhaps a pair of workman's caps?"

"Marcel . . ." The girl shook her head. "Oh, very well, but you and your friend must promise to come back and pay us a purely social call in the future."

"That is a favor we'll be delighted to grant." The Gunsmith grinned.

"*Gut Gott*." Greta smiled. "You're as good at sweet talk as Marcel. I wonder what other talents you have in common."

"You'll find out when we pay you that social call," Clint replied.

"I'll look forward to that," she said, running the tip of her tongue along her lips in a suggestive manner. Then she hurried away to see about the wagon.

"You've got nice friends," Clint told Marcel.

"But of course." The Frenchman laughed. "Why have friends who aren't nice? How do you like my plan?"

"I think it's good," the Gunsmith nodded. "After the meal, we head over to the public urinal—which should seem natural enough—and slip out the side door into the alley. Then we climb into the wagon, don the slickers and caps and ride to Lacombe's den of thieves."

"Exactly," Marcel declared. "Not bad, eh?"

"Of course," Clint added, "if Lacombe's people are watching us, they may not fall for your trick. Even if they do, they'll realize what happened when we don't come out of that urinal after the wagon leaves."

"*Oui*," Marcel sighed. "After all, they must know enough about us to know we wouldn't stay in there for recreation."

"That's about as funny as putting poker chips in a blind man's cup," Clint groaned. "The point is, this trick might help us shake Lacombe's bloodhounds, but not for long."

"Have you got a better idea, *mon ami?*"

"No," the Gunsmith confessed. "If I did, I would have mentioned it by now."

SIXTEEN

All of New Orleans was not comprised of glitter and Old World charm. The waterfront proved to be a collection of tar-roof shacks, run-down warehouses and shanties populated by downtrodden segments of white, black and Indian races who all shared the common trait of hopeless poverty.

The Gunsmith and Marcel Duboir climbed onto the roof of an abandoned warehouse to observe the harbor beyond the slum. With the aid of Clint's Dolland, they watched an assortment of stevedores and *apaches* shuffle up and down the gangplank of *La Reine Rouge* which was docked at the pier.

"I've already seen Lacombe's riverboat," Clint commented. "Where's his casino?"

"Over there," Marcel replied. "To your right."

Through his pocket telescope Clint located a large two-story building with an ornate porch and dark windows. A large sign bore the legend, The Sanctuary, in bold red letters.

"What's it a sanctuary from?" the Gunsmith inquired.

"Morality, decency—who knows?" Marcel shrugged.

"Doesn't seem to have much business going on in there," Clint remarked.

"More than you might imagine," Marcel stated. "But most of Lacombe's gambling profits are made on the riverboat. The police are less likely to raid him when he's miles away in the water.''

''I'm surprised Lacombe worries about the police.''

''The Department of Police is not so bad,'' the Frenchman said. ''Don't judge them all by Lieutenant de Gasquet. For every cop on Lacombe's payroll, there are a hundred others who'd love to see the bastard on his way to prison.''

''Yeah,'' Clint agreed. ''I met Chief of Police John Ryder when I was here in 'seventy-three. He seemed like a pretty good man.''

''Perhaps we should talk to him after we've gotten some evidence,'' Marcel suggested. ''Those stevedores down there are probably hauling stolen merchandise on board *La Reine Rouge* to be taken to illegal traders along the coast.''

''Do you figure that means the riverboat will be leaving port soon?'' Clint inquired.

''Perhaps—'' Marcel began. *''Qu'est-ce que c'est?* What is that shiny object at the starboard side?''

Clint moved the Dolland to scan the length of the riverboat. He saw the bright reflection of sunlight on the lens of a tubular-shaped object which a steward held against his right eye.

''Holy shit!'' Clint exclaimed. ''They've got a telescope too and it's aimed right at us!''

''We'd better get out of here,'' Marcel said urgently.

''Fast,'' Clint added as he watched the steward gesture at the familar figure of Roger Lacombe. The young man turned to glare at the Gunsmith's position.

Clint and Marcel rapidly climbed to the edge of the roof and swung down to the ground. They heard the angry shouting of Lacombe's men and the sound of boots hammering the plankwalk. The Gunsmith and Marcel broke into a rapid run, heading for the alley where they'd left the wagon.

"Oh, goddamn it!" Clint groaned when they reached the mouth of the alley.

The wagon was no longer there.

"Somebody stole it," Marcel commented. "I guess nothing is safe in this neighborhood."

"Yeah," the Gunsmith agreed. "Especially *us*."

SEVENTEEN

A bullet hissed through the air, scant inches from Clint's left ear. He felt its heat as he heard the report of a rifle. The Gunsmith glanced over his shoulder to see one of Lacombe's henchmen closing in fast with a Winchester in his fists.

Clint and Marcel dashed into the alley. Another shot cracked behind them. A bullet smashed into the side of the plaster wall of one of the buildings. The pair ran to the end of the alley and found themselves in the heart of a small fish market.

"Keep going," Clint told Marcel as he positioned himself at the mouth of the alley. "I'll catch up."

Marcel prepared to argue, but he realized there wasn't time for debates. He darted around a fish cart and jogged into another alley. A gunshot echoed from the alley and a bullet splintered the frame of the cart. Bystanders cried out in alarm and fear as they scrambled for shelter.

The *apache* gunman emerged from the alley, trying to work the lever-action of his rifle as he ran. The hoodlum didn't see the Gunsmith until it was too late. Clint pounced from his hiding place at the alley's entrance and quickly seized the man's rifle with both hands.

Clint pulled hard, throwing the *apache* off balance. The hood's fingers slipped from the frame of the rifle as he fell headlong to the ground. Clint still held the Winchester by its barrel. The *apache* rolled over and began to rise, clawing at a revolver in his belt.

The Gunsmith stepped forward and swung the rifle like a club. The hard walnut stock crashed into the thug's face, shattering the cheekbone on contact. The *apache* fell flat on his back. He wouldn't be getting up again for quite a while.

Clint changed his grip on the Winchester and jacked a fresh shell into the chamber. Then he dashed for the next alley to follow Marcel. A bullet whistled somewhere near his back. Clint heard the slug whine when it ricocheted off a mud-brick wall.

He hurled himself behind the cover of the fish cart and fell flat as another shot bit into the wagon. Clint gazed under the cart and saw two more syndicate flunkies moving in fast with pistols in their fists.

Clint assumed a prone position and aimed his rifle around the edge of the cart. He squeezed the trigger. One of the *apaches* cried out as a .44-40 slug slammed into the center of his chest. His body executed an awkward dive backward and fell into Death. The other hoodlum snapped a hasty, ill-aimed shot at the Gunsmith. Clint could only guess where the bullet went because it didn't even come close.

He prepared to return fire, but the thug had turned tail and dashed back to the cover of the alley. Clint couldn't justify shooting the man between the shoulder blades, although he didn't want to let him get away either. He compromised and lowered the aim of his rifle before squeezing the trigger. A bullet tore into the back of the *apache*'s left thigh. He howled in pain and stumbled forward to fall face first against a wall. The city-bred hootowl slumped to the ground, leaving a trail of blood from his crushed nose.

"When do you intend to catch up with me?" Marcel Duboir asked as he appeared beside the Gunsmith.

"I wanted to hold them off for a few seconds to buy us some extra time," Clint explained as he turned to face his friend. "But now—"

His sentence remained unfinished because a burly stevedore with a harpoon in his fists suddenly lunged at the pair. Clint desperately tried to roll over and work the lever of his Winchester. The stevedore charged at Marcel, the wicked steel point of his weapon aimed at the Frenchman's chest.

Marcel ducked low and canted his body aside to avoid the harpoon. His right hand yanked at the handle of his walking stick and a two-and-a-half-foot sliver of steel appeared in his fist. Marcel rapidly thrust the blade into the chest of his burly adversary. The stevedore dropped his harpoon and stared down at the sword which had lanced his heart. He opened his mouth to scream. Blood bubbled from his lips.

"*Au revoir, cochon,*" Marcel hissed as he yanked the sword from the man's lifeless flesh.

The stevedore crumbled in a dead heap by Marcel's feet, but two pistol-packing *apaches* appeared to take the man's place. Both men pointed their guns at the young Frenchman. They failed to notice the Gunsmith until he opened fire. A rifle slug splintered the frontal bone of a gunman's skull. The back of his head blew apart and sprayed bone, brains and blood into the face of his horrified partner.

The second *apache*, shocked by the grisly shower, dropped his gun and raised his arms in surrender. Marcel stepped forward and lunged with his sword. The tip stabbed into the man's right shoulder, the blade sinking deep in his flesh. An agonized howl was ripped from the hood's throat as Marcel pulled his sword free. The *apache* folded at the knees and began to fall. Marcel punched him in the side of the head, his fist still wrapped around the handle of his cane-sword.

Clint rose to his feet and worked the lever of his Winchester as another stevedore charged forward, swinging a huge steel hook overhead. The Gunsmith aimed at the man's chest and squeezed the trigger. The hammer clicked when it fell on an empty chamber.

"Shit!" Clint rasped as the stevedore advanced.

The Gunsmith quickly raised the rifle, using the frame as a bar to block the assassin's attack. The hook rang against the barrel of the Winchester. Before the stevedore could launch another assault, the Gunsmith's boot lashed out and caught the man squarely between the legs.

A choking gasp came from the stevedore's trembling lips. He staggered on weak legs, his arms falling to his sides, hook dangling loosely in his fist. Clint swung the Winchester and butt-stroked his opponent as hard as he could. Three teeth spewed from the man's mouth as he fell unconscious.

The thunder of numerous footsteps and excited voices warned them that more of Lacombe's legions were about to arrive. Clint and Marcel dashed into the nearest alley as half a dozen armed men poured into the fish market. The Gunsmith and his partner ran into a shanty consisting of crudely erected lean-to tents. Hollow-eyed faces fearfully gazed up at them as the pair jogged between the tents and headed for the sturdier shelter of the brick and wood structures in the distance.

Suddenly, two figures appeared in their path. The Lacombe hirelings aimed revolvers at Clint and Marcel. The Gunsmith lowered the empty rifle and shrugged his shoulders in defeat.

"Don't shoot," he said with a sigh. "We surrender."

He tossed the Winchester aside as if to confirm his remark. The gunmen followed the rifle with their eyes. They were distracted for less than a second, but long enough for the Gunsmith to draw his .45 Colt. The revolver roared and a bullet drilled a gory hole between the eyes of an *apache*.

Before his companion could respond, the other hoodlum discovered he had troubles of his own. Marcel had rapidly swung his right arm, hurling his sword in an underhand throw. The sharp tip of the steel blade struck the *apache* in the solar plexus and pierced upward into his heart. The gunman convulsed in agony, his finger pulling the trigger of his pistol to blast a harmless round into the ground.

"You sure know how to get your point across," the Gunsmith commented.

"This fellow seems to have taken it to heart," Marcel replied as he yanked his sword from the dead man's chest.

"We'd better talk about this later," Clint urged.

"*Oui*," Marcel agreed, sliding his sword into the cane scabbard. He relieved one of the dead men of a pistol.

"About time you got a gun," Clint declared as he glanced over his shoulder.

The Gunsmith didn't like what he saw. Four members of the Lacombe syndicate were approaching fast. Two men carried rifles while the others shuffled forward, burdened by a large tubular shaped weapon with numerous muzzles gaping from its multibarreled frame.

"Jesus," Clint muttered. "They've got a Gatling gun."

"They wouldn't dare use it here around all these people," Marcel said, but his words lacked confidence.

"You willing to bet your life on that?" the Gunsmith

commented as he ran for the larger structures beyond the shantytown.

"No," Marcel admitted, galloping after Clint. "But it was a nice thought."

They reached the buildings as rifles cracked behind them. Hastily fired bullets hissed past Clint and Marcel. The Gunsmith glanced back at the pursuers to see that the *apaches* had placed the Gatling on a tripod mount.

The Gunsmith quickly seized Marcel's arm and pulled him toward an alley. The pair dashed through the opening as the Gatling gun thundered insanely, spraying a volley of rapid fire projectiles. Bullets sung sour sharp notes as they bounced off the brick frames of the buildings.

"*Merde alors!*" Marcel exclaimed when he stared at the end of the alley.

A brick wall blocked their path. Boxed in by three solid walls, the Gunsmith and Marcel would be chopped to pieces by the Gatling gun.

EIGHTEEN

Lacombe's hoodlums cheered in victory when they realized Clint and Marcel had fled into a blind alley. The *apaches* scrambled into a better position for the kill and aimed the Gatling at the mouth of the alley.

The Gunsmith glanced around and saw a door, the side entrance of one of the buildings. He quickly took aim and fired two rounds into the wood near the knob. Marcel slammed a foot into the door and it swung open.

Clint and Marcel ducked through the open door. The metallic rattle of the Gatling gun exploded a salvo of murderous projectiles which hissed and whined as they ricocheted off brick. A couple of stray rounds bit into the doorframe, splintering wood.

"Christ," Marcel gasped breathlessly. "That was too close."

"*Too* close is dead," Clint corrected.

They'd entered a room filled with shelves of multi-colored bolts of cloth and populated by faceless mannequins. A long table in the center of the room held an assortment of dressmakers' tools, including scissors, a pin cushion and dress patterns.

"We appear to have stumbled upon the workshop of a lady's boutique," Marcel observed.

"If we can get to the front room," Clint began, "we might be able to sneak out of here and slip away from Lacombe's bastards before—"

The Gunsmith fell silent when a door swung open. A blond woman clad in a lacy white dress appeared at the threshold. Although she was a stunning beauty with sky-blue eyes, a pert nose and a tempting mouth nicely filling an oval-shaped face, the nickel-plated revolver in her fists immediately caught the men's attention. The girl tumbled back the hammer.

"Drop your guns," she ordered, repeating the command in French.

"We don't want to hurt you, lady," Clint assured her. He raised his hands, the modified Colt still in his right fist.

"I told you to drop your guns!" she snapped angrily.

"*Mademoiselle, s'il vous plaît*—" Marcel began.

"I won't tell you again," she insisted. "You *apache cochons* have gone too far when you break into my home and place of business!"

"Hell, lady," Clint replied. "We're not *apaches*, for chrissake. Gaston Lacombe's gunmen are trying to kill us and that's why we had to bust into your place."

"Lacombe?" she asked with surprise. "You are his enemies, *oui?*"

"You think he'd be trying to gun us down if we were buddies?" the Gunsmith countered.

"All we ask is that you allow us to leave via the front door, *mademoiselle*," Marcel told her.

"They have probably sent someone around front already," the girl warned. "Come with me."

She lowered her pistol and the men did likewise. They followed her into a magnificent dress shop where dozens of beautiful lace and silk dresses were displayed on lifelike dummies complete with glass eyes and wigs. The girl led them behind a counter and pointed to a narrow flight of stairs.

"You'll find a trap door to the roof," she instructed. "Need I say more, *messieurs?*"

"Indeed not." Marcel grinned. *"Merci, ma beauté."*

He mounted the steps while Clint turned to the girl. "What's your name?" he asked.

"Marie Labou," she replied.

"You're as brave as you are lovely, Marie," he declared. "Thank you."

Then he followed Marcel up the stairs.

They popped open the trap door and climbed onto the slate-tiled roof. From the roof cresting, they had a clear view of the streets below. Three *apaches* were still stationed by the Gatling near the alley. At the other side of the boutique, they saw a pair of gunmen creeping toward the main entrance.

"Think you can take those two?" the Gunsmith inquired softly.

"I can but try," Marcel replied as he awkwardly thumbed back the hammer of the Remington .44 he'd confiscated from one of the slain *apaches*.

"Better try real hard," Clint told him.

The Gunsmith crawled along the roof peak to a dormer while Marcel slithered to a stone chimney. Clint gripped the gable board of the dormer with his left hand and leaned against the corner board as he aimed his Colt at the trio by the Gatling gun.

He stared down the barrel of his revolver. When the front sight bisected the head of one of the hoodlums, Clint squeezed the trigger. The Colt barked harshly and the *apache* fell backward, both hands clamped over his bullet-gouged face.

The remaining pair of gunmen looked up at Clint as he rapidly fired his double-action weapon. Another member of Lacombe's goon squad was kicked into the Hereafter by a .45 slug in the chest. His partner fumbled with the Gatling gun, trying to adjust its aim to open fire on Clint. He was far too slow and a bullet in the side of his head made him far too dead to present any further threat.

Clint heard Marcel's Remington boom three times. He turned to see the young Frenchman clinging to the chimney with one hand as he slowly lowered his weapon from eye-level, extending his arm as he aimed in the manner of a duelist. He fired one more shot.

"Did you get them both?" the Gunsmith asked.

"*Oui*," Marcel replied happily. "The first one didn't even know I was on the roof until I put a bullet into the top of his head. The other fellow was more difficult. I must confess, I missed him twice and one of his bullets came close enough to make my heart visit my throat. But, when the *bâtard* broke cover and tried to bolt across the street, I finally nailed him."

"Good work." Clint nodded. "I don't see any more of Lacombe's stooges. Maybe they've retreated back to the boat."

"We killed more than a dozen of the slime," Marcel declared. "They'll think twice before they come after us again."

"They'll think twice all right," Clint said grimly. "And return with as many men as possible. Let's not hang around and find out if they've got any more surprises like that Gatling gun. I wouldn't put it past these sons of bitches to show up with a cannon next."

"Oui, mon ami," Marcel agreed. "We might put our pretty ally in danger as well as ourselves if we remain here for long."

"I don't think she's too worried about that," the Gunsmith remarked. "But *I* am."

NINETEEN

"Did you kill them all?" Marie asked as Clint and Marcel descended the steps.

"We got the team that was trying to kill us," Clint answered. "But Lacombe has lots more where they came from."

"*Oui*," she agreed sadly. "It seems there is no end to the minions of *apaches* under that devil's command."

"You seem to have a personal quarrel with Lacombe," the Gunsmith commented.

"Perhaps I do," she replied stiffly.

"I'm going to look about the street to see if any of the *cochons* are hiding in a nook or cranny out there," Marcel announced as he headed for the door.

"I didn't mean to pry, Marie," Clint told the girl.

"And I did not mean to act in such a defensive manner toward a man who has finally struck an effective blow against Lacombe's syndicate."

"It's just a beginning," the Gunsmith stated. "But we have to start somewhere."

"You'll need more than two men to do battle with the Devil, *monsieur*."

"Call me Clint," the Gunsmith said. "We know what the odds are, Marie. Right now, two men are the best we can do. Maybe if you know some other folks who are tired of paying protection to Lacombe, we can form a strong resistance and fight back in number.''

"Everyone is tired of living in fear, Clint," she said wearily. "But few will risk their lives to fight what frightens them."

"What about you?" Clint asked. "Do you want to fight?"

"I hatc Lacombe," Marie told him. "I want to see him dead more than I want my own life. If I thought I could succeed, I'd find that bloody *bâtard* and kill him myself. The only thing that stops me is the knowledge I would never get close enough to do so. Too many of his people know me."

"Sounds like you had a pretty bad run-in with Lacombe."

"My husband refused to pay for protection," Marie explained. "So they killed him. I went to the police and we confronted Lacombe with an accusation of murder. I should have known it would not be that easy. Lacombe denied everything, of course, and challenged the police to produce some sort of evidence against him. Police Chief Ryder told me his department could not risk a charge of false arrest. Lacombe has powerful friends at City Hall, *oui?*"

"I've met Ryder," Clint stated. "That was a few years ago and I can't say that I knew him very well, but he seemed like the sort of lawman who wouldn't just roll over and quit."

"He didn't," Marie answered. "He continued the investigation and tried to get some proof to indicate Lacombe's involvement. However, a week after my husband was murdered, a policeman named Sergeant de Gasquet claimed to have captured the killer. He said he found a Chinese breaking into a haberdashery on Rue

Marché. The Chinese supposedly pulled a gun and de Gasquet was forced to kill him. As the Oriental died, his last words were a confession of the murder of Pierre Labou.''

"How convenient," Clint muttered. "Didn't anyone question what motive this Chinese may have had to kill your husband?''

"Apparently the man was an opium addict," the girl said. "No one even knew his name.''

"Since he was Chinese, no one probably cared," the Gunsmith commented. He'd seen the bigotry and hatred that many whites have toward the Chinese. Oriental customs, culture and language seemed very different to them. People tend to fear what they don't understand.

"Sergeant de Gasquet was considered quite a hero after that," Marie said bitterly. "They promoted him to lieutenant.''

"I know." Clint sighed.

"Later, Lacombe sent me a message stating that he regretted my husband's death and he hoped I'd come to my senses about his involvement in the murder. His *apaches* never returned to this boutique to try to collect protection money again.''

"They were probably ordered to leave you be," the Gunsmith mused. "Ten to one, Lacombe realized you'd refuse to pay and you'd be apt to put a bullet in anyone he sent. If you killed one of his boys or they killed you, it would cause more trouble than it would be worth to the syndicate.''

"True," Marie agreed. "After all, Lacombe had already murdered Pierre and gotten away with it. That proved to be an ample lesson to the other shopkeepers who might wish to rebel against the syndicate.''

"Clint," Marcel called from the doorway. "We'd bet-

ter be on our way before Lacombe sends a battalion of
apaches after us.''

"What about Marie?'' the Gunsmith demanded.
"They might think she was helping us from the start.''

"She'll have to tell them that we broke in and forced her
to show us where the trap door to the roof is,'' Marcel
replied.

"But will they believe her?'' Clint frowned.

"They won't believe it unless they see some evidence
that I did not willingly assist you,'' Marie stated simply.

The Gunsmith stared at her. "What do you mean?''

"Hit me,'' she told him.

Clint winced. "I can't do that. . . .''

"You have to,'' Marie insisted. "If I'm not bruised
they'll be suspicious.''

"She's right, Clint,'' Marcel said. "And Lacombe's
people will beat the hell out of her if they think she might
be an ally.''

"Shit,'' the Gunsmith muttered.

His arm swung in a short arch, his open palm smacking
Marie across the left cheek. Her head snapped to the side
from the blow. Clint's stomach knotted up, angered and
disgusted by being forced to strike a woman—especially
one he found both attractive and admirable.

"Clint,'' Marie said with a sigh, "you didn't slap me
hard enough to kill a fly. Try again.''

"Christ,'' the Gunsmith hissed through clenched teeth.

The back of his hand lashed out, striking the girl on the
side of the face hard enough to spin her around. Marcel
suddenly lunged forward and grabbed her arms. He ripped
a sleeve of her dress at the shoulder and slapped her again,
sending the girl stumbling into Clint's arms.

"Damn it, Marcel!'' the Gunsmith snarled.

"We have to get out of here, Clint," the Frenchman declared sternly. "I'm sorry, *mademoiselle*."

"No need to apologize," Marie assured him in an unsteady, breathless voice. "What you did was for my sake. *Merci, mon ami*."

Clint looked at her face. Both cheeks were red and a trickle of blood crept from the corner of her mouth. Marie's eyes were moist with tears. A cold hard fist gripped at Clint's guts. He took her into his arms.

"Marie," he began, "when this is over, I'd like to take you to dinner and show you how I usually treat a lady."

"When this is over." She smiled up at him. "Now, be on your way. *Bonne chance*."

TWENTY

"Zut!" Jean-Paul LeTrec exclaimed after listening to the Gunsmith and Marcel Duboir recalling the incident at the harbor. "You two have stirred up a hornets' nest this day! *S' il plaît à Dieu,* Lacombe does not make us all suffer for your actions!"

"If you ask for God's will," Yves Materott said sharply, "then ask that He help us fight these *athées cochons!"*

"Oui, Monsieur Materott," Henri Duboir agreed. "What is done can not be changed. What matters is my son and Clint have returned uninjured and many of Lacombe's *apaches* will never threaten us again."

The Gunsmith listened to the other men discuss the matter. He shook his head. Clint and Marcel had returned to Henri's house to find LeTrec and Materott waiting in the parlor. Two of the local businessmen who had been victimized by Lacombe, they had agreed to meet with the Duboirs and Clint to discuss future strategy against the syndicate.

"Gentlemen," Clint began. "I trust you're all aware that Lacombe has had this house watched. He's been able to keep track of our activities without much trouble so far. This conference might well put all our lives on the line."

"Is this so, Henri?" a horrified LeTrec demanded.

"It is quite possible, *oui,"* the senior Duboir admitted.

100

He cast a sharp look at the Gunsmith, clearly angered by Clint's remark.

"They have a right to know what they're up against," the Gunsmith stated.

"Lacombe could kill us for this!" LeTrec cried. "He might be burning down my house at this very minute!"

"You should have warned us, Henri," Materott complained.

"But we have to meet somewhere to organize a proper resistance against Lacombe," Marcel told them.

"We did not have to meet here," LeTrec insisted. "You and this outsider who calls himself *L'armurier* may have led the *apaches* straight back here!"

"I don't call myself the Gunsmith in any language, friend," Clint declared. "And no matter where we held a meeting, we'd be taking the same risk. You men ought to know by now that Lacombe has all of you under surveillance to some degree."

"In other words," LeTrec said fearfully, "the syndicate is too large, too well organized to fight!"

"If you want to surrender to blackmail, that is up to you," Henri told him.

"Better to pay Lacombe to leave us be than to fight him and be wiped out," LeTrec declared. "Our homes, businesses and families could suffer if we try to resist."

"You don't reward a man for stealing from you," the Gunsmith stated.

"That is easy for you to say, Adams," LeTrec replied. "You have nothing to lose in this."

"Clint risked his life for us," Marcel snapped. "That's something of personal value he could lose, is it not?"

"A gunfighter must not value his life very highly," LeTrec sniffed. "Who can say what motivates such a man?"

"I'm not a gunfighter," Clint told him. "But I'm sure getting sick of hearing you snivel like a spoiled brat, fella."

"Oh, so you would threaten to shoot me?" LeTrec demanded. "You are no different from Lacombe and his *apaches*, Adams!"

"I'm going to throw your ass out of my father's house," Marcel said simply as he approached LeTrec.

"Let's all calm down," Henri urged. "Marcel, don't expell *Monsieur* LeTrec . . . just yet."

"It would appear we now have to choose one of two actions," Materott commented. "Either we surrender to Lacombe's extortion or we fight him tooth and nail. I favor the latter, but you must give us some hope to succeed in such a battle."

"Okay." Clint nodded. "But first, I want to know if you're really concerned about the safety of your families or if you two are just plain cowards."

"How dare you insult me!" LeTrec hissed.

"Because I haven't seen any evidence that you're really a man, LeTrec," Clint answered.

"I will not sit here and listen to this," LeTrec fumed as he rose from his chair.

"Go ahead and leave," the Gunsmith told him. "But if you decide to turn informer for Lacombe and help that son of a bitch against us, you'd better hope he kills me before I find out."

LeTrec stared at Clint and swallowed hard.

"Marcel," Henri said softly. "I believe it is time for you to see *Monsieur* LeTrec to the door."

"*Oui*, Papa," Marcel replied with a wolfish grin.

"You are all making a mistake—" LeTrec began.

"Marcel," Henri interrupted sharply. "If our guest

does not shut his mouth, you have my permission to kick in his *balloches* before you throw him out the door.''

LeTrec hastily turned and hurried to the exit.

''I guess that tells us what we can expect from Le-Trec,'' Clint commented. ''How about you, Materott?''

''I am not a gunman, *Monsieur*,'' the shopkeeper replied. ''So, I must ask that you remove your gunbelt if you intend to call me a coward. Then I will try to beat the shit out of you. *Comprendez?*''

''That means you either want to fight me or you want to fight Lacombe,'' Clint said. ''Which is it?''

''I am not a coward,'' Materott declared. ''Tell me how we can fight the syndicate and win. I'll follow you only then.''

''Tomorrow morning,'' the Gunsmith began, ''I'm going to see Police Chief John Ryder. I know him. Ryder isn't the sort to be on a gangster's payroll. He's familiar with Lacombe's syndicate. If we can get enough evidence against those bastards, I'm sure Ryder will help us.''

''Lacombe has friends in City Hall,'' Materott warned.

''So I've heard.'' Clint smiled. ''But politicians are only good at *keeping* a fella out of trouble. They're not too good at *getting* anyone out of it except for themselves. Lacombe's pals among the New Orleans high mucky-mucks will disown him the minute he's hauled into jail.''

''What about his *apaches?*'' Materott asked.

''Clint and I killed a dozen of Lacombe's scum-for-hire,'' Marcel stated happily. ''They're not really as formidable as you seem to think, *monsieur*.''

''But Clint Adams is an expert with a gun,'' Materott remarked. ''And you, my dear Marcel, you have always been a little crazy.''

''*Oui*,'' Marcel shrugged. ''But the two of us were still

too much for Lacombe's men.''

"The next few days are going to be very unpleasant,''
Clint warned. "You and everyone else who decides to
fight will have to turn your homes and businesses into
fortresses. You'll have to prepare areas of shelter and arm
yourselves. Sentries will be posted to alert your local
militia when and if Lacombe's men arrive.''

"If they try to shake down one shop,'' the Gunsmith
continued, "every one of you must be ready to come to
your neighbor's aid. You'll need to decide the best points
to set up riflemen to get the *apaches* in a crossfire without
exposing your own men. You'll have to be ready to shoot
to kill. It's a hard choice, but there isn't any other way
unless you want to live under Gaston Lacombe's thumb.''

"We'll fight, *Monsieur* Adams,'' Materott said firmly.
"We should have done as you say long before now.''

"Yeah,'' Clint agreed. "You should have. I saw a
horse and buggy and a buckboard out front. Which one
belongs to you?''

"The wagon is mine,'' Materott replied.

"Why don't you give me a ride over to your section of
town and we can start making preparations now?'' the
Gunsmith suggested.

"Very well.''

"Shall I come with you, Clint?'' Marcel asked.

"Better stay here,'' the Gunsmith answered.
"Lacombe knows about you and Henri. This house is the
most likely target for an attack.''

"I have André and Phillippe,'' Henri Duboir said.
"They'll protect me if anything happens.''

"Ah!'' Marcel smiled. "Could it be you do not want
me to come along for a different reason, Clint?''

"How's that?'' the Gunsmith inquired.

"Perhaps you plan a private rendezvous with the charming young lady we met earlier today?"

"Figured I might rent a horse from one of Materott's friends and maybe take a ride over there to see how she's doing," Clint admitted.

"But of course." Marcel grinned. "You're such a considerate fellow."

"That's a fact."

TWENTY-ONE

Clint Adams spent more than three hours with Materott and other shopkeepers at Rue Trois, helping them organize a neighborhood militia. Then he borrowed a leather apron and a stocking cap from a butcher and a horse from a livery stable. Soon he was on his way back to the harbor.

The Gunsmith didn't care much for his mount. He was accustomed to riding Duke, who was a remarkably intelligent and dependable horse. The cross-breed Morgan-Mustang Clint rode to the harbor didn't respond well to commands from a stranger. It tried to bite the Gunsmith, which earned the animal a punch on the muzzle. After that, the horse grudgingly obeyed its rider.

When he arrived at the boutique, Clint tied the horse to a hitching rail. The animal snorted sourly. *Same to you, fella*, the Gunsmith thought. He was relieved to see a light in the front window as he walked to the shop and knocked on the door. It opened a mere crack.

Marie Labou's lovely face appeared in the opening. Clint noticed she had her nickel-plated pistol in hand. He removed the cap to be certain she'd recognize him.

"Have you gone into a new line of work?" Marie asked with a grin, glancing down at his leather apron.

"I keep trying to just be a gunsmith," Clint said, "but I keep getting sort of sidetracked into other things."

"Come in," she invited, holding the door open wide.

The Gunsmith entered. He was relieved to see that her shop hadn't been crudely ransacked by Lacombe's men. Everything appeared to be the same as it had been earlier that day. Marie didn't seem to have suffered at the hands of the *apaches* either. A faded bruise on her cheek was all that marred her beauty.

"Did Lacombe's goons pay you a visit after we left?" he asked.

"A very brief visit, thank God," she replied. "Roger Lacombe and some of his brother's pet apes burst in here and demanded to know what happened. I told them two men had broken into my store and knocked me down. Naturally, I stayed down until the shooting was over. The two men left via the front door. I claimed that this was all I knew."

"Did they believe you?" the Gunsmith inquired.

"I think so," Marie nodded. "When Roger said he and the others were searching for you, I asked if you were enemies of Lacombe. He told me you were so I said I hadn't helped you two, but if I'd known you were against the syndicate, I would have gladly done so."

Clint whistled softly. "That wasn't very smart. They might have hurt you for a remark like that."

"Oh"—she shrugged—"Roger punched me in the stomach. It didn't feel very good, but it was worth it to tell the *bâtard* what I think of him."

"Damn it, Marie!" Clint snapped. "I thought we were trying to keep you from getting hurt."

"Is that why you came back?" Marie inquired. "To see if I was all right?"

"Yeah," he said, trying to sound convincing.

"Was that the *only* reason?" she challenged.

"Not really," Clint admitted.

He stepped forward and embraced Marie. Her arms snaked around his neck. Their lips met gently, tongues exploring the rims of each other's mouth. The kiss gradually became more passionate. Their mouths pressed harder and tongues dove and probed fiercely. Clint's hand wandered to Marie's breast, feeling her nipple harden under his touch.

The girl gently moved his hand. "Put out the lamp," she whispered.

Clint moved to the lantern. He raised the globe and turned down the fuel valve. Marie moved to another room, shedding her clothes as she walked. The Gunsmith blew out the lamp flame and followed her.

Marie had led him into a bedroom. She already stood naked by the edge of a brass-framed bed as Clint unbuttoned his shirt. Marie sat on the mattress and watched him remove his trousers. The Gunsmith slipped out of his long johns and crossed the room to join her on the bed.

In the darkness her skin seemed very pale, but the shapely curves of Marie's perfect figure were also clearly visible. Clint ran his fingers over the soft, warm flesh of her breasts. His hands traveled down her bare body as his mouth found her nipples. He kissed and tongued them gently. The pink tips hardened in his mouth as he drew on them.

Clint's touch moved to her sleek, flat stomach and slowly crept lower. His lips shifted to the girl's belly while his fingers stroked her long smooth thighs. Gradually, his head lowered to the blond triangle between her legs. The musk scent of her womanhood filled his nostrils like a primitive perfume. Clint's tongue lapped at her moist chamber of love. His teeth tenderly pried at the lips of her vagina as his tongue sunk deeply inside.

Marie moaned with pleasure. Clint then took her by the

shoulders and eased the girl's back against the mattress. He climbed on top of her, putting his weight on his elbows. Marie's groping hands found his erect manhood and steered it into her damp, warm womb.

The Gunsmith felt the marvelous, erotic thrill of penetrating a new lover for the first time. His penis slid into the fleshy portal as Marie gasped in passion. Clint rotated his hips slowly to ease himself deeper. There was no hurry. Love prolonged is love fulfilled.

He didn't begin to thrust harder until he felt the girl's desire reach its boiling point. She trembled beneath him, her nails raking his flesh. Clint rammed himself harder and faster. Marie wrapped her legs around him and bucked and squirmed mightily. The Gunsmith groaned as he felt his seed explode. Marie cried out with delight. She too had climaxed.

"Oh, God," the girl whispered. "I have not made love for many months. I had almost forgotten how wonderful it can be."

"Let's make sure you remember tonight for a long time, Marie," Clint urged.

"Oh, I'm certain I will," she replied sincerely.

TWENTY-TWO

Although Marie invited Clint to spend the night, he decided it would be best for him to get back to the Duboir house. After they'd made love three times, Clint climbed out of bed and pulled on his clothes.

"When we've finished with Lacombe," he began, sliding his .22 New Line Colt inside his shirt, "we'll get together again."

"When it's over." Marie sighed. "I wonder if it will ever be over."

"The syndicate is in for one hell of a fight," the Gunsmith declared. "Trust me."

"I do," she assured him. "But I also know what Lacombe can be like. Be careful, Clint."

"You too," he said, strapping on his gunbelt.

"You—" she began awkwardly. "You'll be going back West afterward, won't you?"

"That's right," Clint stated. "I won't make any promises that I don't intend to keep, Marie. Anything we have together will be temporary."

"Not if we remember it afterward," she remarked. "It can live in our hearts forever, *oui?*"

"Yes," he agreed. "It sure can."

An unexpected crash, accented by the snapping of broken wood, suddenly drew the Gunsmith's attention to the front room. He dragged his Colt .45 from leather as the sound of footsteps warned that intruders were rapidly approaching the bedroom.

"Get down on the floor and try to find some cover," Clint told Marie.

An explosion of shattering glass behind the Gunsmith made him whirl to face the bedroom window. He caught a glimpse of a man's head and shoulders. The barrel of a rifle jutted through the jagged hole in the broken window-pane.

Clint's revolver roared. Orange flame lit up the room for a fragment of a second. The face at the window was instantly transformed into a mask of pulverized, scarlet flesh. The gunman fell from view.

"Drop the gun, Adams!" a voice hissed. "Or we'll splatter you all over the walls!"

The Gunsmith turned slowly. Roger Lacombe and Jules stood in the doorway. The junior Lacombe aimed a British-made .45 caliber Tranter at Clint Adams. Jules was armed with his sawed-off Smithers shotgun. Even the Gunsmith couldn't beat a combination like that.

Perhaps he could take them with him to Boot Hill. Clint's double-action revolver allowed him to fire with incredible speed and his own skill and reflexes might be enough to kill both Roger and Jules. Still, one of them would get off a shot—probably Jules. The big man didn't have to be good with a gun, not with the sort of wide, devastating buckshot pattern that a scattergun spews out.

If they'd intended to kill the Gunsmith, they'd simply gun him down right there and then. Clint decided to play the odds and hope a better chance would arrive later. He tossed his .45 onto the bed and raised his hands in surrender.

"So the great *L'armurier* does not wish to die bravely after all," Roger snickered.

"We were told to take him alive if possible," Jules reminded Roger. "Your brother said he'd prefer a captive to a corpse."

"I know," the young Lacombe muttered. "I only hope we can make his death a slow and painful one after Gaston has questioned this Anglo *cochon*."

"That's what I like about you, Roger," Clint said dryly. "You're such a worthless little shit, you make everybody else look great in comparison."

"I'm going to enjoy cutting you up a little at a time," Roger hissed angrily. "I'll skin you alive, Adams. I'll have a necklace made of your teeth and your eyeballs for my cufflinks. Perhaps I'll cut your balls off and have them made into a coin purse, eh?"

"So you can have an excuse to fondle them?" Clint laughed. "You little queer."

"La vache!" Roger snarled as he stomped forward, ready to use his pistol as a club.

Suddenly, Marie leaped up from the floor and reached for Clint's discarded Colt on the mattress. Roger lunged forward and seized the girl by the hair. She screamed as he yanked hard and hurled her across the room. Clint resisted the urge to attack Roger, well aware Jules still had a shotgun aimed at his belly.

"I'm so glad we found you, you little bitch," Lacombe spat as he gathered up Clint's gun and shoved it into his belt. "You lied to us earlier today. For that you will pay, trollop!"

"Merde!" the girl replied, glaring at Roger.

He responded by slapping the back of his hand across her face. Marie staggered into a wall. Roger's leg lashed out and swept her feet out from under her. Marie fell to the floor. He kicked her in the breast. The girl cried out and clutched her chest.

This was too much for the Gunsmith to bear. He lowered his arms and prepared to lunge for Roger Lacombe, ready to beat him to death with his bare hands. Pure savage fury overcame Clint Adams. He was too filled with rage to remember his .22 belly gun or even to consider Jules's shotgun. He wanted to kill Roger Lacombe personally. For those few seconds, Clint was a wild beast that wanted to taste the blood of his prey.

However, Jules had already grabbed Roger and pulled the young barbarian away from Marie before he could cause her further harm. The Gunsmith dove for Lacombe, his hands aimed at Roger's throat. Jules swung his right leg in an incredibly fast roundhouse kick. The steel foot slammed into Clint's left shoulder.

The Gunsmith was abruptly hurtled into a corner by the power of the kick. He slumped to the floor, breathless. His left arm was numb. Jules limped closer and aimed the twin muzzles of his scattergun at Clint's face.

"We have wasted too much time already," Jules growled. "Get up, *Monsieur* Adams, or we will be forced to kill you and the young lady this very minute. *Comprendez-vous?*"

TWENTY-THREE

"Put this on," Roger ordered as he yanked a blue gingham dress from the closet and tossed it at Marie.

"I must get some underclothes," she replied weakly, still rubbing her bruised breast.

The girl moved toward a dresser and reached for the top drawer. Clint wasn't certain, but he guessed Marie's pistol was hidden there.

"We haven't got time for that," Roger insisted. "Just put on the dress or we'll drag you out of here naked."

"We don't need her anyway." Jules shrugged.

"That's right," Clint Adams agreed. "So just leave her be. I'm the one you want."

"*Oui*." Jules nodded. "That is why I think we should kill her."

The Gunsmith stiffened. "Kill her? What for?"

"You must think we are stupid, Adams," Roger chuckled. "This little *vache* would go squealing to the police if we let her go now. True, we have many policemen on our side, but others have yet to be enlightened. We must either take her with us or kill the bitch. Which shall it be?"

Marie made the choice. She slipped into the dress.

When Clint and Marie were escorted outside at gunpoint, they discovered a carriage waiting for them in the street. The rig resembled a fancy stagecoach painted red and yellow. The Gunsmith and Marie were shoved inside.

Jules entered and pointed his scattergun at Clint while Roger wrapped an arm around Marie's neck and pressed the muzzle of his Tranter revolver against her head.

"Try anything," he warned, "and I'll kill her."

The Gunsmith still found himself unable to take any action against his captors. Cursing his helplessness, Clint rode in silence as the carriage rolled forward. He tried to formulate an escape plan, but he couldn't do anything until an opportunity arrived that would make such effort feasible instead of merely suicidal.

The trip was brief. The carriage had taken them to the pier where *La Reine Rouge* was still docked. Clint, Marie and their captors emerged from the vehicle and marched up the gangplank.

Gaston Lacombe and Baccarat stood at the port side. The syndicate leader leaned on the handrail and smiled at the Gunsmith. Baccarat appeared to be bored by the arrival of the prisoners.

"Welcome once again to *La Reine Rouge*," Gaston greeted. "And this time, you didn't even have to pay for a ticket, *Monsieur* Adams."

"Wonderful," the Gunsmith muttered. "Now what do I have to pay to get off this tub?"

"That is what we must discuss," Gaston replied. "I trust you remember Baccarat? I had thought she might be interested in seeing you again, but it seems she would rather go back to bed."

"Really, Gaston," Baccarat said with a sigh. "This has been a very tiresome day already. Must it be a tiresome night as well?"

"You are not pleased to see Clint Adams again, *ma cherie?*"

"Adams?" Baccarat frowned. "I vaguely recall his face, but I did not remember this man's name."

She stared at the Gunsmith. For a tenth of a second, Baccarat's eyes adopted a pained expression as if to say, "I warned you. Why didn't you listen?" Then she shrugged.

"Is he important, Gaston?" Baccarat inquired.

"So far he has been a pest," Lacombe answered. "After we talk, Adams will either be an ally or a corpse. Jules, bring our guest."

"*Oui, Monsieur,*" the brute said as he poked Clint in the back with his shotgun.

Gaston glared at Marie. "Why did you bring her?"

"She was a witness," Roger replied.

"Don't you know how to handle such problems?" the older brother demanded. "The dead cannot bear witness to anything."

"She is a friend of Adams." Roger grinned. "A *very* close friend."

"Probably just a tart he was spending the evening with and—" Gaston suddenly took a closer look at Marie. "Ah! So it is you again! The little dressmaker who caused such an uproar a while back. You should have considered yourself fortunate when I decided to let you have your petty little boutique after you tried so hard to cause me trouble."

"You killed my husband—" Marie began.

"And soon you will join him," Gaston told her.

"She helped Adams, Gaston," Roger stated. "She may be able to tell us more about the Duboirs and the citizens' militia."

"Neither of which will be a problem for us much longer." Gaston shrugged. "I've already seen to it that the old judge will be dealt with. As for the shopkeepers . . ."

He turned to gaze at a row of kegs at the port quarter.

The Gunsmith read the black printing on the kegs. It was kerosene.

"Their resistance will go up in smoke tomorrow,", Gaston concluded. "Still, the girl may have something of interest to tell us. We can also use her to cross check information from Adams."

"I'll question her, Gaston," Roger said eagerly.

The older man laughed. "Very well, my brother. Entertain yourself with the lady while Adams and I discuss business."

"Jesus Christ," Clint Adams hissed as he turned to face Lacombe. Jules dug the barrels of his Smithers into Clint's ribs.

"That's right, Adams," Gaston replied. "At this moment, I am Jesus Christ and God Almighty because I hold the power of life and death over you. I can be your salvation or send you to Hell with a snap of the fingers. And now, *monsieur*, let's talk."

TWENTY-FOUR

Gaston Lacombe led Clint into his plush office cabin once again. The Gunsmith followed him inside, Jules still at his heels with the Smithers held ready. Lacombe strolled to his desk and sunk into the leather chair behind it. He looked up at Clint and sighed.

"Do you remember the last time we met in this very office, Adams?" Gaston inquired. "We were friends on first name terms. We shared some French brandy and I offered you a job, which you refused."

"You didn't give me any idea how much money you were talking about," Clint answered as he sat in the chair across from Lacombe.

"We never discussed a salary." Gaston shrugged. "You did not ask about it. You simply said no."

"Look," the Gunsmith began, "your offer didn't appeal to me for two reasons. First, your dear brother hates my guts. I don't think I'd want to turn my back on him for long."

"And the other reason?"

"Your offer sounded like a plain old job as a strong-arm boy who happens to use a gun instead of muscle. There wouldn't be enough money in that for me. See, I only work short-term jobs. If I can't make a bundle of cash in a few days, I'll go somewhere that I can."

"And I am to believe that the Duboirs made you a better

offer?'' Gaston shook his head. ''Do not insult my intelligence, Adams.''

''Apparently you don't know about Marcel Duboir,'' the Gunsmith replied, making up the story as quickly as his agile mind would allow. ''He was in Europe for a year and a half.''

''I am aware of that.''

''But did you know he returned to New Orleans a very wealthy man?'' Clint inquired.

''Wealthy?'' Gaston raised his eyebrows. ''How wealthy?''

''Enough to offer me three thousand dollars to help fight you. For that kind of money, I'd go into Hell and kill the Devil himself.''

''How did Marcel make this fortune?'' Lacombe asked suspiciously.

''Damned if I know,'' Clint told him. ''And damned if I care. So long as I get paid, I don't ask questions.''

''I think you're lying to me, Adams,'' Gaston declared. ''When we met in your hotel room, you seemed fiercely loyal to the Duboirs. Why have you changed your mind?''

''I figured the odds were in their favor.'' The Gunsmith shrugged. ''Hell, do you think they told me the truth about how big your operation was? I didn't realize what I was up against until we got in that fight with your boys this afternoon.''

''You and Marcel Duboir killed a dozen of my men,'' Gaston told him. ''And you killed another one tonight.''

''What choice did I have?'' Clint demanded. ''They were trying to gun me down so I shot them first. What do you think I should have done? Just let the bastards blow holes through me?''

''You still seemed too devoted to the Duboirs and their absurd crusade.''

"Well, the judge saw to that," Clint hissed through his teeth. "You see, I'm wanted for the murder of a federal marshal in Texas. That's why I had to get out of the Lone Star State double-quick. A riverboat to New Orleans was the fastest way to lam out a long ways without having to worry about a posse."

"You could have gone to Mexico."

"I ran into a little trouble down there too," the Gunsmith replied. "And the *federales* have long memories about that sort of thing. I don't speak Spanish very well and this scar on my cheek makes me too easy to recognize. No way I'd head to Mexico. The lucky fellas down there are the ones that only have to face a firing squad."

"I've never heard of the Gunsmith getting into trouble with the law," Gaston remarked. "Except for that business several years ago when the Army thought you were selling guns to the Comanches. They dropped the charges as I recall."

"Yeah." Clint smiled. "I sure buffaloed those blue-bellies."

"So you *were* selling guns to the Indians?" Gaston raised his eyebrows once more.

"Quanah Parker paid in gold," Clint lied smoothly. "And he paid well."

"Let's say you did kill a federal marshal in Texas," Gaston began. "You fled to New Orleans to avoid a hangman's noose. Since my riverboat does a lot of business around Galveston, that might explain why you'd refuse to work for me."

"That's right," Clint agreed, wishing he'd thought of that excuse before Lacombe had.

"But it doesn't explain why you agreed to help the Duboirs," Gaston concluded.

"Well, three thousand dollars is one reason," Clint answered. "And Judge Duboir had heard about my trouble in Texas. He told me he could pull some strings and get the charges dropped if I helped him. Otherwise, he'd turn me over to the federal authorities in this state and have me sent back to Texas."

"Why didn't you simply kill the judge?"

"Wouldn't be that easy," Clint insisted. "He wrote up a statement about me and put it in a safe-deposit box in a bank. If he dies, the box will be opened and I'll be suspected of murdering that old fart as well as wanted for gunning down a Texas lawdog. I don't want to have to run to Alabama next. After a while, I'll start running out of states to haul ass for."

"I'm not certain I believe you, Adams," Gaston commented as he rose from his desk and walked to the liquor cabinet. "You might be telling me the truth . . . or you might be trying to save yourself."

"Or I might be doing both at the same time," the Gunsmith said, glancing over his shoulder at Jules. The bodyguard was stationed by the door, his shotgun dangling toward the floor in a loose grip.

"Even if you are telling the truth," Gaston began as he poured himself a glass of brandy, "I really don't see any reason to let you live."

"I'm good with a gun," Clint told him, slipping his hand inside his shirt. "You've already seen enough proof of that."

"Indeed." Lacombe chuckled. "Enough proof to know you could still be very dangerous to me if I allowed you to join my ranks only to discover your loyalties are still with the Duboirs, *oui?*"

"Not a gambler, eh?" Clint asked as he rose from his chair, careful to keep his back to Jules as he drew the Colt

New Line belly gun from its hiding place.

"No, I'm not," Lacombe replied as he turned from the liquor cabinet with a balloon glass in his hand.

His eyes widened in fear as he stared into the muzzle of Clint's .22 which was suddenly thrust into his face.

"Well," the Gunsmith said simply, "*I am.*"

TWENTY-FIVE

The Gunsmith heard the hammers of Jules's shotgun click as the big man cocked his weapon. Clint took a deep breath and stepped closer to Gaston Lacombe. If Jules intended to pull the trigger, he'd have to do it before Clint was too close to the syndicate boss or the wide pattern of buckshot from the scattergun would kill Lacombe as well.

Jules held his fire.

"Tell him to put the shotgun on the floor and kick it over here," the Gunsmith instructed Gaston as he moved behind the ringleader to use Lacombe for a shield.

"You're a fool, Adams," Gaston declared. "You'll never get off this boat alive."

"That'll make two of us," Clint replied, poking the muzzle of his New Line Colt against the back of Lacombe's skull. "Now, tell him to put down that gun."

"Jules," Gaston began, his voice remarkably steady under the circumstances, "do as he says . . . for now."

The burly bodyguard hesitated, unwilling to surrender his weapon. Clint quickly wrapped his left arm around Lacombe's throat and pressed his pistol against the gangster's temple to be certain Jules would see the immediate threat to his employer's life.

"Put down the gun or I'll kill him," the Gunsmith announced. "If that happens, you'll be working for

Roger. Somehow, I don't think you two would get along very well. What do you think, Jules?''

The big man uncocked his Smithers and placed it on the floor. He glared at Clint and said, ''I think a better time will come so I can kill you without endangering the life of *Monsieur* Lacombe.''

''Hope springs eternal,'' the Gunsmith replied. ''Kick that scattergun over here.''

Jules's steel foot clanged against the barrels of the Smithers and the shotgun slid across the floor to the Gunsmith.

''Good boy,'' Clint said. ''Keep it up and you'll earn yourself a new collar and leash. Now, walk over to the wall, raise your hands and lean against the wall. Keep your hands high and your nose close enough to the wallpaper to be able to tell me what it smells like.''

Jules continued to obey the Gunsmith. He assumed a spread-eagle position, facing the wall. Clint swapped his New Line Colt from his right hand to his left and suddenly shoved Gaston Lacombe, sending the kingpin staggering across the room.

''Your turn, Lacombe,'' Clint declared. ''Same position as Jules, but you get acquainted with the door. Try to touch the knob or call out, you'll get a bullet in the spine.''

Gaston also followed instructions. Clint quickly gathered up the sawed-off Smithers. He pocketed the diminutive .22 pistol and held the shotgun ready as he approached the pair. Clint moved behind Jules.

''Don't move a muscle,'' he warned. ''I'm going to frisk you.''

''*Cochon bâtard*,'' Jules hissed fiercely.

''Same to you, fella,'' Clint replied as he swung the Smithers.

The heavy steel barrels crashed into Jules's skull hard.

The bodyguard's forehead bounced off the wall. He slumped to the floor unconscious at the Gunsmith's feet.

"That ought to keep your watchdog out of the way for a while," Clint told Lacombe. "Now, you and I are going to leave here together. First, we find out where your brother took Marie. Then all three of us—the girl, you and me—are leaving this boat together. Understand?"

"I understand," Gaston answered. "But obviously you do not understand that you've already sealed your own fate. You're a dead man, Adams."

"Not yet, Lacombe," Clint told him, jabbing the twin muzzles of the shotgun into the small of Gaston's back. "Let's go."

Lacombe opened the cabin door and they stepped into the corridor. Fortunately, the hall was empty. Clint kept the Smithers at Gaston's spine.

"Where would Roger take Marie to 'question' her?" he asked.

"Probably to his cabin," Gaston replied.

"Would you figure he'd want to be alone with her or is it likely he has a helper?"

"Roger would rather do things with a lady in private." Gaston shrugged. "Wouldn't you?"

"Yeah," Clint said. "But I'm not a yellow-bellied young rattler with a gutsy lady who'd like to scratch my eyes out."

"Roger will have the girl in restraints," Gaston stated. "He has rather creative tastes in sexual activities."

"What the hell does that mean?" Clint demanded.

"Roger has ropes and gags in his bedroom."

"And whips too, I bet," the Gunsmith hissed. "Get me to that son of a bitch's cabin—*fast*."

"It's only a few doors down the hall," Gaston assured him as he led Clint through the corridor.

They reached the door to Roger's cabin. Clint ordered Gaston to knock. The gangster leader rapped on the door. Roger's voice angrily told his visitor to go away.

"It's me, Roger," Gaston barked at the door. "I have to talk to you. Open up."

"*Merde!*" the younger brother exclaimed as he yanked the door open.

Clint shoved Gaston into his brother. Both Lacombes stumbled across the length of Roger's cabin. Clint followed right behind them. He trained the shotgun on Gaston and Roger, allowing himself a brief glance around the room.

The cabin furniture consisted of a small table, two armchairs, a chest of drawers and a bed. Marie was located on the latter. Her dress was torn and a dark bruise surrounded her left eye. Roger had tied her wrists and ankles to the four posts of the bed. The girl lay spread-eagle on the mattress, a gag wrapped around her mouth.

Clint kicked the door shut. Roger still had the Gunsmith's double-action .45 revolver in his belt. The young hoodlum prince fumbled for the gun, but froze when he stared into the twin muzzles of the Smithers sawed-off in Clint's hands.

"Give me an excuse, you bastard," the Gunsmith told him. "I'd love to splatter your rotten carcass all over this room, so go ahead and draw that gun."

"Don't shoot, Adams!" Roger pleaded. "I'm just taking the gun out of my belt to give it back to you."

He eased the revolver out and stooped to place it on the floor. Roger shoved the gun with a palm and slid it over to Clint. The Gunsmith glanced at Marie's battered face.

"You goddamn . . ." he began, but he couldn't think of an insult that equaled the contempt and rage he felt for Roger Lacombe.

The Gunsmith closed in rapidly while Roger was still bent over. Clint's leg lashed out. The heel of his boot smashed into Roger's face, crushing his mouth. The youngest Lacombe brother skidded across the floor until he bumped into a wall.

Gaston Lacombe surprised Clint. The Gunsmith hadn't expected the kingpin to personally attack him. Gaston lunged forward and seized the Smithers, trying to twist the shotgun from Clint's grasp.

The Gunsmith rammed a knee into Gaston's soft belly. Lacombe groaned in pain and Clint took his left hand from the shotgun long enough to form a fist and punch his opponent in the side of the head.

Gaston fell backward and landed abruptly in a seated position in one of the armchairs. During the struggle, the shotgun slipped from both men's fingers and fell to the floor between them. Clint ignored it. He stepped forward and swung a powerful right cross to the point of Gaston's jaw.

The punch knocked the ringleader backward, tipping over the chair. Man and furniture crashed to the floor and lay still. Clint heard a muttered curse in French and turned to see Roger was on his feet once more.

Blood drooled from the youth's torn lips, but the hatred in his eyes revealed that he still had plenty of fight left. Roger snarled like a wild animal and slashed a shoe at Clint's groin. The Gunsmith dodged the kick and quickly grabbed Roger's ankle with both hands.

Clint twisted Roger's leg and threw the young hoodlum off balance. Roger fell to the floor forcibly and Clint moved in, prepared to stomp the punk's face into the carpet. One of Roger's legs swept at Clint's ankles, attempting to trip him. The Gunsmith hopped backward in time to avoid the kick, but Roger quickly rolled to the discarded .45 revolver nearby.

The youth's hand closed on the frame of the double-action Colt. He slithered on his belly, panting hard as he swung the pistol at the Gunsmith and thumbed back the hammer.

"Now, I send you to Hell, Adams!" he snarled.

Roger pulled the trigger. . . .

TWENTY-SIX

The explosion of the Colt within the cabin seemed to rattle the entire room. A .45 caliber lead missile hissed past the Gunsmith, tugging at his left shirt sleeve and grazing flesh as Clint desperately dove to the floor.

He landed beside the sawed-off Smithers shotgun. Clint grabbed the weapon and shifted the barrels to point at Roger Lacombe. The startled youth was unaware he held a double-action revolver in his fist, so he wasted time cocking the Colt.

The Gunsmith was much faster. He slapped back one of the hammers of the Smithers with his left palm and immediately squeezed the trigger with his right index finger. The shotgun roared as if Hell itself had blasted its way into the room.

A swarm of buckshot pellets struck Roger Lacombe in the face and shoulders. Clothing, flesh and muscle were shredded by the shotgun blast. Roger's features vanished and the top of his skull burst in a shower of gore. Clint's modified double-action revolver slipped from the dead man's limp fingers.

"You lost your head for the last time," the Gunsmith muttered as he rose to approach the corpse.

Since there was only one shell left in the shotgun, Clint retrieved his .45 Colt before he hurried to the bed and untied the bonds attached to Marie's right wrist. The girl pulled the gags from her mouth.

"Thank God," she gasped. "I don't know what that lunatic would have done to me if you hadn't—"

"Talk later, honey," the Gunsmith urged. "We're right in the middle of a nest of rattlesnakes and all those two-legged sidewinders are going to be racing down here in about five seconds. Can you manage to free yourself now?"

"I think so," she replied, already untying the knots of the rope fastened to her left wrist. "What do we do now?"

"We hope all of Lacombe's men figure they can't get along without him," Clint told her as he strode across the room to the dazed figure of Gaston Lacombe.

The hoodlum kingpin groaned as he regained consciousness. Clint heard the thumping of footfalls overhead and the unintelligible murmur of numerous voices from the corridor beyond. Soon, fists pounded on the cabin door. Lacombe's men shouted questions in French, which the Gunsmith didn't understand. Still, he didn't need a translator to know the men outside were asking about their boss. And when they didn't get an answer, they'd break down the door to find out why.

Clint's suspicion proved prophetic. The door burst open and three hard-faced *apaches* appeared at the threshold, all armed with pistols. The Gunsmith stood beside Gaston Lacombe. His .45 Colt was aimed at the gangster's head and the Smithers shotgun was pointed at the doorway. The *apaches* froze in their tracks and stared in total bafflement at Clint.

"Back off," the Gunsmith told them. "Otherwise I start shooting. I'll kill your boss and I'll take a few of you with me before I die as well."

The hoods gaped at the big muzzles of the shotgun and

the glassy-eyed face of Gaston Lacombe. They still weren't sure what to do.

"I've got nothing to lose if you don't back off," Clint warned. "If I'm gonna die, I won't die alone. If you think I'm blowing smoke, call my bluff and let's all meet Our Maker together."

The *apaches* muttered a jumbled assortment of expressions in French and English. Clint caught the term *L'armurier* and a few obscenities in both languages. Then a figure dressed in a steward uniform appeared at the door. Clint recognized the man named Debray.

"We cannot allow you to kill *Monsieur* Lacombe," he declared simply.

"Then get everybody out of the corridor," Clint replied.

Gaston sat up, rubbing his jaw gingerly. Debray gazed down at his boss. *"Monsieur?* Are you harmed?" the henchman asked.

"No," Lacombe told him. "I'm all right. Adams! Where is—?"

"Right here," Clint told him, cocking the hammer of his Colt for effect.

"And Roger?" Gaston asked sternly.

"He's dead," Debray explained.

Gaston stiffened for a moment and glanced about. He gasped in horror when he saw the mutilated, decapitated corpse of his brother. For several seconds, he knelt before the Gunsmith and trembled in anger and grief. Clint was surprised Roger's death affected Gaston to such a degree. The Gunsmith found it difficult to believe anyone could have liked a worthless piece of human scum like Roger Lacombe—even if he had been Gaston's brother.

"Don't let Adams get off this boat alive," Gaston hissed in French.

Clint knew what the gangster leader had said because Marie translated the sentence for him. The girl had untied herself and joined the Gunsmith.

"Better think twice about that, Debray," Clint told the henchman. "With Roger dead, you guys can't afford to lose Gaston as well. I'm sure none of you dumb bastards have connections with City Hall. How long do you think you'll be able to operate the syndicate without Lacombe? How long will your friends on the police force be willing to help? They'll turn on you faster than a rabid dog in order to save themselves from exposure."

"We cannot allow you to kill *Monsieur* Lacombe," Debray repeated. "But we cannot permit you to kidnap him either."

"Let's compromise, Debray," Clint suggested, guessing that the henchman was a survivor who'd be willing to make a deal with Satan's personal attorney if it served his own interest. "You fellas let us get off the boat and give us a couple of horses and a headstart and we'll leave Lacombe for you."

"Alive and unharmed?" Debray inquired.

"You have my word," the Gunsmith agreed.

"Debray!" Gaston snapped. "Don't listen to this murdering *bâtard!*"

"I believe *Monsieur* Adams will keep his word," Debray declared. "We must save your life, *Monsieur* Lacombe. For now, that is all that matters."

"My brother's death must not go unavenged!"

"*Oui.*" Debray nodded. "Tomorrow we will return to war with Adams."

He turned to face the Gunsmith. "This is only a reprieve," the henchman stated. "What we call *sursis à statuer*—a stay of execution. We will hunt you down and kill you, but not tonight."

''Just business,'' Clint smiled. ''I can understand that, Debray. You've got a deal.''

The henchman nodded in agreement.

TWENTY-SEVEN

Clint Adams checked the corridor. It was deserted. He turned to Marie Labou and handed her his New Line.

"You might need this," he told her. "It's a close-quarters weapon. You won't hit much beyond ten feet and don't count on stopping anyone with just one bullet, but if somebody gets within six feet or so, this little baby will do the job. Okay?"

"I understand, Clint," she assured him. *"Merci."*

"It's time to go, Lacombe," the Gunsmith told the hoodlum king. "Am I going to have to kick you in the ass to get you out the door?"

"I'll walk," Gaston assured him. Lacombe's hands were now bound behind his back and he'd recovered his confidence and dignity. Clint was certain Gaston was now determined to stay alive—and equally determined to have his revenge.

"Just for the record," Clint said. "I killed your brother in self-defense. He took a shot at me first. I didn't have any other choice."

"Even if I believed you," Gaston replied, his eyes ablaze with hatred, "it would not matter. It would not change a thing."

"Then I don't give a shit if you believe me or not. But it still happens to be the truth. Let's move."

Lacombe led the way, followed by the Gunsmith with

the Smithers sawed-off pressed against Gaston's spine. Marie brought up the rear, watching the corridor for a possible ambush attempt from behind.

So far so-so, Clint thought. *But what are things like topside? My word is good, but how good is Debray's word? Does Jules outrank Debray? If he's recovered consciousness, he might have canceled the deal I made with Debray. . . .*

"The hell with it," the Gunsmith muttered under his breath. "We'll find out in a minute anyway."

They mounted the steps of the hold and emerged on deck. The trio stepped onto the wooden surface at the starboard side near the stern. Several of Lacombe's men were lined up by the bow, staying several yards away. None of them held weapons in view.

"It looks like Debray is keeping his word," Marie commented.

"Maybe," Clint replied. "I can't believe all those guys would be willing to put away their weapons so eagerly. Let's see what happens when we—"

The Gunsmith caught a glimpse of movement— perhaps a shadow on the deck or a flapping shirt sleeve from the corner of his eye. Later he wouldn't be able to recall exactly what warned him as he turned to see two figures leap from the flybridge.

Clint raised the shotgun by pure instinct and squeezed the trigger. A ball of amber fire burst from the last barrel of the Smithers. One *apache* was struck full in the chest by buckshot. His airborne body hurtled backward and landed somewhere on the bridge. The other assailant cried out in agony, but his body continued forward.

The *apache* fell into Clint Adams. Both men toppled to the deck. The Gunsmith felt wet, sticky blood from the ragged remains of the man's right arm. Buckshot had nearly severed the limb below the elbow. The wounded hoodlum attempted to wrestle the shotgun from Clint's grasp, but the Gunsmith easily pushed him away.

Marie aimed the New Line at the injured man's head and fired a .22 into the side of his skull. The *apache* dropped to the deck and quietly died. Clint scrambled to his feet, drawing the modified .45 Colt as he rose.

Gaston Lacombe had taken advantage of the distraction and fled. The Gunsmith hadn't even caught a glimpse of the escaping syndicate boss, but he saw plenty of Lacombe's hoodlums closing in fast. The *apaches* had drawn their pistols from beneath their jackets and quickly moved in for the kill.

"Honor among thieves," Clint growled. "Bullshit!"

He rapidly fired three double-action .45 rounds at the advancing gang members. Two *apaches* tumbled backward, falling into their comrades. Men ran for cover, firing hasty, poorly aimed rounds at Clint as they fled. The two wounded hoods were left to twitch out the remnants of their lives before their bullet-torn hearts ceased to function.

Clint heard the familiar *pop-crack* of the New Line. He glanced over his shoulder to see Marie holding the tiny gun in both hands. She fired upward at a rifle-toting shadow on the flybridge. The *apache* groaned and staggered. Clint blasted a .45 into the ambusher which knocked him off his perch. The man did an awkward dive—headlong to the deck.

A trio of *apaches* charged Clint's position from the starboard quarter. The Gunsmith snapped off another shot and one of the attackers caught a bullet in the face. The man was dead by the time he crumpled to the deck. His partners immediately retreated.

Bullets sizzled past the Gunsmith's head. None of the

apaches seemed to be very good with a gun and they weren't accustomed to fighting anyone who shot back at them. Terrorizing shopkeepers wasn't the same as trading lead with the Gunsmith. However, Clint had no illusions about the odds. There were too many of them to try to fight. Sheer numbers alone put the battle in their favor.

"Over the side," he told Marie. "Fast!"

"What?" she asked, startled by his remark.

Clint didn't waste time repeating himself. He grabbed the girl's arm and pulled her as he ran to the handrail. The Gunsmith fired his last round at the *apaches* to try to buy another second or two of time.

Marie understood. She grabbed the handrail and hauled herself over it. Clint heard the splash when her body dropped into the water below. He jammed the empty Colt into his belt and prepared to join her.

A bullet splintered wood near his hand as he grabbed the rail. Fear increased his speed and he leaped over the barrier like a mule deer being chased by a cougar. Shadows flashed past his eyes as he plunged through the darkness.

He hit the water feet first and felt the clammy cold engulf his body. Clint dropped under the surface and swam in a low breaststroke, kicking his legs like a frog. He didn't come up for air until he was unable to hold his breath a moment longer.

Clint heard the reports of firearms in the distance. He blinked his eyes to clear them and glanced back at the boat. The Gunsmith was astonished when he realized how far he'd managed to swim in so short a period of time. The men on board *La Reine Rouge* would have been just as surprised. They were firing their weapons at the water near the boat, unaware that their quarry had managed to swim more than fifty yards from the vessel.

"Clint!" Marie's voice called. The girl splashed through the water toward the Gunsmith. "Thank God! I thought we were going to die back there."

"Back there or right here," the Gunsmith commented, "dead is still dead. Let's keep moving before Lacombe's people figure out what happened."

"Where are we going?"

"Somewhere dry," Clint replied as he swam for shore.

TWENTY-EIGHT

Clint and Marie swam to a pier some distance away from *La Reine Rouge*. They spied a trio of rowboats docked under the plankwalk, tied to the pillars supporting the pier. The couple climbed into one of the vessels, grateful to be out of the cold wetness, and concealed from view if any of Lacombe's men patroled the harbor.

"*Zut*," Marie whispered through chattering teeth. "I was warmer in the water."

"I know what you mean," the Gunsmith agreed, trembling in the night breeze. "But we'd better hide here for a while before we try to row this thing somewhere else."

"Where?" Marie asked.

"Northeast," Clint replied. "From there we'll be able to head for a friend's house. It's the only safe place I can think of."

"Safe?" Marie frowned. "Where in New Orleans can we be safe from Lacombe's syndicate?"

"Trust me," the Gunsmith urged, taking her hand in his.

"Oh," she began, returning Clint's .22 New Line Colt. "This belongs to you. I managed to hold on to it after I jumped overboard."

Clint smiled. "Good work, Marie. Hey, you handled yourself just fine back there."

"I was too scared to do otherwise." She grinned.

He broke open the loading gate of the New Line. There were two unused cartridges in the cylinder, but they might not be reliable after being soaked in water. Clint didn't have any spare ammo for the New Line or his .45 Colt. He'd have to dry and clean the weapons the first chance he got and reload them with his ammo supply at the Duboirs' house.

"I'm freezing," Marie complained. "We can't stay in these wet clothes with this chill. We'll catch pneumonia."

"We don't have any dry clothes to change into." The Gunsmith sighed.

"No." Marie smiled. "But we can take our clothes off and get warm."

Clint stared at her, startled by her remark. They were still in the enemies' territory, yet she was suggesting they strip down and make love right under Lacombe's nose. It was too absurd to even consider.

Yet, Clint's eyes wandered over her face and body. The wet tattered dress clung to her lovely frame, hugging the curves of her breasts. Her eyes were filled with fierce passion. It seemed to infect the Gunsmith. A fire began to kindle within his loins as well.

"What the hell," he muttered as he unbuttoned his shirt.

They shed their clothing and placed it in one of the other rowboats. Marie lay on her back, her shoulders braced against the seat. Clint mounted her carefully, placing his knees on the hard wood floor. She hooked her legs around his hips as he entered her.

The gentle rocking of the boat seemed to assist the Gunsmith's thrusts. Marie bit into his shoulder to muffle her groans of pleasure. Clint drove himself deeper and increased the tempo of his lunging manhood. Marie's teeth dug into his flesh painfully as a wild orgasm made her body quiver.

The Gunsmith had never experienced anything quite like this before. It was desperate lovemaking because both realized it might well be the last time to share their passion. The incredible risk and danger involved made it even more exciting. It was foolish, insane and wonderful.

TWENTY-NINE

Three hours later, the Gunsmith and Marie Labou had reached Rue Croissant. They'd spent more than an hour under the pier before they'd wrung out their clothing as best they could and rowed to the northeast. Then they'd walked through shadows and alleys for two more hours until they'd finally approached Henri Duboir's house.

Shivering in their still damp clothing, the couple opened the front gate and walked to the judge's home. The Gunsmith was too tired and cold to notice that neither Andre or Phillippe, Henri's bodyguards, met them at the door. However, when he saw the splintered wood of the doorframe near the lock, Clint knew what had happened.

"Jesus," he rasped. "Lacombe told us that the Duboirs would be dealt with. His goddamn *apaches* have already been here!"

"Maybe they're still inside the house," Marie said fearfully.

"And maybe Henri or Marcel need help," the Gunsmith replied.

He shoved the door open, slamming it back against a wall. Clint stood clear of the doorway in case an assassin waited within the house with a gun or knife. Neither a bullet nor a blade whistled toward him in response, so the Gunsmith cautiously entered.

Clint dragged the empty .45 from his belt. Trying to bluff with a useless weapon wasn't his style. Bluffing at a

142

poker table is one thing, but the same tactic when one's life is at stake is potential suicide. Still, he didn't have any alternative.

He found one of the bodyguards in the front room. The burly, bearded figure lay on the floor, his shirt soaked with blood. The leather-wrapped haft of a knife protruded from his chest, the blade buried in his heart. Marie nearly choked as she stifled a scream.

"It's André or Phillippe," the Gunsmith whispered. "I never learned which name belonged to which man."

"Maybe he isn't—" the girl began.

"He's dead," Clint said simply.

The Gunsmith didn't upset Marie by mentioning the fact that the murder weapon appeared to be a throwing knife. Clint had never favored bladed weapons, but he knew enough about knife-throwing to realize a hurled dirk doesn't usually penetrate deeply enough to kill. The assassin or assassins had probably thrown the knife into the guard's chest and then pulled the wounded man to the floor where they drove the blade in deeper as one might a tent peg.

The dead man's shotgun was gone and Clint didn't see any evidence that the bodyguard had managed to fire his weapon before the assailants killed him. *Poor bastard,* Clint thought. What had been his last thoughts as the *apaches* pinned him to the floor and hammered the knife into his heart? Terror, anger or bitter failure that he had died before he could strike a blow against the enemy?

"I should have learned your name," the Gunsmith whispered as he slid two fingers over the dead man's eyelids to close them.

They found the other bodyguard in the parlor. Unlike his partner, he had gotten a chance to fight back. The man's thickset body was covered by scarlet stripes—

bloodstains from numerous knife wounds in his back and chest. Another man lay beside the dead bodyguard, his neck twisted at an unnatural angle, face staring lifelessly up at the ceiling. Clint didn't see any wounds on the *apache*'s corpse.

"Good for you, Phillippe or André," Clint remarked. "You got one of the bastards."

"What did he do to him?" Marie asked, staring down at the bodies in fascinated horror.

"Lacombe's hootowls stabbed our friend to death," the Gunsmith explained. "But before he died, he managed to break this fella's neck."

Clint led Marie to the stairwell leading to the next story. A pair of legs dangled above the steps. The girl clamped her hands over her mouth when she gazed up at the figure that hung from the end of a thick hemp rope tied to a railing above.

The Gunsmith recognized the gray-haired man who'd been hanged in his own house. Henri Duboir's face was purple and his tongue jutted from the corner of his open mouth. His eyes bulged from their sockets, the terror of his final moments of life engraved on their pupils.

"Goddamn you, Lacombe!" Clint Adams spat angrily.

His rage was useless and only served to drain him of what energy he had left. Clint sat on the stairs and shook his head helplessly.

"Goddamn you," he croaked hoarsely, burying his face in his hands.

THIRTY

After disassembling the double action .45 Colt and the New Line belly gun, Clint Adams dried every part of the firearms with a cloth. Then he applied a thin layer of oil and reassembled the guns. Satisfied both pistols were in perfect working order, he loaded the cylinders.

"Shouldn't we contact the police?" Marie inquired, watching the Gunsmith insert cartridges into his weapons.

"Better wait till dawn," Clint replied. He'd retrieved a spare gunbelt from his gear. He buckled it around his waist as he spoke. "I don't want to report this business to anyone except Chief Ryder. We're going to tell him about this personally."

"What about . . . them?" Marie tilted her head toward a door which led to the kitchen. Clint had dragged all four corpses into the room.

"They'll just have to keep until then," the Gunsmith told her.

"This is terrible," she said sadly. "This whole thing has been one long nightmare."

"Not *all* of it." Clint grinned.

"No," Marie agreed. "Making love to you has been wonderful. It has helped me keep my sanity."

"Never thought of it that way," The Gunsmith shrugged.

"Clint, we don't have to wait here in the parlor," Marie began. "Perhaps we could go upstairs to one of the bedrooms?"

"Lord give me strength," Clint whispered, resisting an urge to roll his eyes toward the ceiling.

The sound of a door creaking on ill-treated hinges suddenly arrested their attention. Clint heard footsteps in the front room. He unsheathed his .45 as he headed for the door.

"Go upstairs and wait until I call you," he whispered to Marie.

"Clint—" she began to protest.

"Go on," he insisted. "I checked out the house and you'll be safe up there. You'll find a Springfield carbine in my room if you need it."

"I'd rather use your bed," she purred, kissing his cheek. "With *you* in it."

"Later, baby," the Gunsmith replied.

Marie was lovely, charming and as brave as any man, but Clint was getting frustrated with her desire to have sex when there was a good chance a gunfight could erupt at any moment. However, she headed for the stairs at last and Clint moved to the front room.

Three figures dressed in blue uniforms with brass buttons on their tunics stood in the center of the room. They stared down at some bloodstains on the carpet. Two of the policemen were strangers to the Gunsmith, but he recognized the third—Lieutenant de Gasquet.

"You guys want to buy that rug?" Clint inquired as he approached the trio. "You'll have to talk to Marcel about it when he gets back. Henri isn't able to make business transactions anymore."

The lieutenant and the other cops turned sharply and

stared at the Gunsmith. They gaped at the pistol in Clint's hand.

"Do you intend to assault three police officers with a deadly weapon, *Monsieur* Adams?" de Gasquet demanded.

"You fellas ought to knock before you enter somebody's home," Clint told them as he holstered his sixgun. "Just because you're police, that doesn't give you any right to barge into a place like this."

"But we are here on official business," de Gasquet declared. "We are investigating a report of a disturbance here. Quite possibly, a violent disturbance. *Oui?*"

"Is that a fact?" Clint asked, glaring at de Gasquet. "And just who made this report?"

"You are in no position to ask any questions, Adams," de Gasquet replied.

The lieutenant stepped aside to reveal that the two officers with him had drawn a pair of S&W .32-caliber pocket pistols. They cocked their weapons as they pointed the guns at the Gunsmith's chest.

"Clint Adams," de Gasquet began in a smug, authoritative voice, "You are under arrest for the murder of Judge Henri Duboir and the two bodyguards who were in his service."

"You bastard," Clint muttered as he raised his hands. "How do you explain the fourth corpse?"

"A hapless stranger who you also killed in your murderous berserk rage." De Gasquet smiled. "And you are also charged with attempting to assault three police officers in the execution of their duty. These two men are my witnesses."

"*Oui*, Lieutenant de Gasquet," one of the cops agreed.

"So all three of you work for Lacombe." Clint sighed.

"I should have guessed that. Maybe you guys killed Henri and the others too."

"That is an absurd accusation, *monsieur*," de Gasquet remarked as he cautiously moved behind the Gunsmith and plucked the modified Colt from Clint's holster.

"Yeah," Clint snorted. "I doubt if you fellas actually stabbed Phillippe and André or strung up Henri, but I wouldn't be surprised if you walked up to the door in your nice blue uniforms and got the guards to open the door. Maybe you held them at gunpoint until Lacombe's goons could arrive. . . ."

"Do you honestly think a jury will believe this non-sense, Adams?" De Gasquet chuckled.

"We'll see who they believe, fella," the Gunsmith answered.

"That suits me, *monsieur*," the lieutenant agreed. "Outside we have a large wagon we call a *panier* which means a basket, but we use it to transport criminals such as yourself. You will now come with us and enter the *panier* so we can take you to jail. *Oui?*"

"Do I have a choice?" the Gunsmith muttered.

"But of course." De Gasquet laughed. "You may very well be shot when you try to escape."

THIRTY-ONE

The policemen escorted Adams outside and marched him to a large black paddy wagon with two fat gray horses hitched to the rig. Lieutenant de Gasquet drew the Gunsmith's own Colt from his belt and aimed it at Clint. One of the patrolmen also covered the prisoner while the third cop put his gun away to produce a ring of keys from another pocket.

"Are you guys really going to take me in with that cock-and-bull story for an excuse?" Clint inquired.

"No," de Gasquet replied. "But as soon as Officer Tailleur unlocks the door to the *panier*, you will try to flee and Officer Jante and I will be forced to shoot you dead."

The Gunsmith only had one choice of action. He'd have to try to draw his belly gun and start shooting. It was a hopeless, desperate move. The crooked cops would certainly gun him down, but maybe he could die fighting. . . .

"*Bonsoir, cochons,*" a voice whispered from overhead.

The startled policemen looked up to see a shape suddenly leap down from the roof of the paddy wagon. Officer Tailleur dropped the keys to the vehicle and fumbled for his gun while de Gasquet and Jante tried to train their weapons on the unexpected assailant.

A long leg shot out from the airborne shadow. A shoe

149

smashed into Jante's face before he could fire his pistol. The kick made Jante's head snap back sharply a moment before his entire body hurled to the ground in a senseless heap.

Clint didn't wait to see what might happen next. He whirled and chopped the bottom of his fist down on de Gasquet's wrist to knock the Colt from the cop's grasp.

The Gunsmith immediately followed up with a left hook to de Gasquet's jaw. The lieutenant staggered backward two steps, but Clint kept coming and drove an uppercut to de Gasquet's solar plexus.

The corrupt lawman started to double up. Suddenly, his left arm flicked out and jabbed a fist into Clint's chest. The Gunsmith almost stumbled off balance, but managed to keep his footing. Lieutenant de Gasquet cursed under his breath and launched a vicious kick at Clint's midsection.

The Gunsmith blocked the kick with his left forearm and managed to scoop up the attacking leg at the knee. Surprised, de Gasquet threw a right cross at Clint's head. Clint caught the cop's wrist with his free hand and quickly pulled de Gasquet forward. The Gunsmith bent his knees to haul the lieutenant across his shoulders.

''Merde alors!'' de Gasquet cried out in alarm.

Clint straightened his knees and raised the cop's horizontal body to shoulder level. Then he turned sharply and hurled de Gasquet to the pavement. The lieutenant's back slammed against the street forcibly, knocking the wind from de Gasquet.

The Gunsmith didn't take any chances with his opponent. He folded a knee and dropped on top of the stunned cop, his bent knee landing squarely in de Gasquet's breadbasket with all his weight behind it. The lieutenant uttered a choking groan and Clint punched him on the chin with a solid right. With a sound that could have been a sigh of relief, de Gasquet's body fell limply unconscious.

Clint glanced up to see his rescuer nimbly parry a punch from Tailleur. The tall man slipped under the cop's arm and hooked a knee into Tailleur's gut. The last of the trio of crooked lawmen doubled up from the blow. His adversary grabbed the stunned officer and rammed Tailleur's head into the paddy wagon. The policeman slumped to the ground with an abbreviated groan.

"Your timing is terrific, Marcel," Clint told his rescuer.

"When I saw de Gasquet and his men step from this *panier* and approach the house, I guessed there would be trouble," Marcel Duboir replied with a smile.

"Why did you hide on the roof of the wagon?" the Gunsmith asked.

"How was I supposed to get inside it?" Marcel shrugged.

"Marcel," Clint began slowly, "have you been home lately?"

"I left shortly after you departed with Materott," the young man explained. "I decided to go pay Greta's brother for the buckboard we lost at the harbor. I sort of got involved with the girls and I didn't get back until just now. . . ."

Marcel fell silent when he saw the grim expression on Clint's face. The Gunsmith took a deep breath.

"They killed your father, Marcel," he said quickly, hoping it would make the announcement less difficult.

It didn't.

THIRTY-TWO

Police Chief John Ryder hadn't changed much since the first time Clint Adams had met him. Ryder was a short, portly man who still wore a full mustache, muttonchop sideburns and three-piece suits. Perhaps there was a little more gray in the chief's hair and his eyes may have acquired bigger bags under them, but otherwise he didn't seem much different.

"My God." Ryder sighed. "It's Clint Adams. Just what I frigging needed!"

"You were more pleasant when I visited you a few years ago," the Gunsmith commented as he entered Ryder's office.

"Well, I didn't know what a hornets' nest you were going to stir up at the time," Ryder answered. "And you never told me what was behind that business with Paul Martel."

"I had to leave New Orleans sooner than I'd expected." Clint shrugged.

"Oh, I remember that you went into the bayou," Ryder stated. "You might recall that I found that female guide—she called herself Andy as I recall—to lead you through the swamps."

"I remember Andy." The Gunsmith nodded.

"Do you also remember that I was in charge of the investigation of the disappearance of Paul Martel and his wife Michelle? What about the explosion that leveled Martel's house?''

"You'd like some answers, eh?"

"I certainly would," Ryder insisted. "You and Andy went into the bayou shortly after someone tried to kill you. Neither of you ever contacted me again."

"I'm here now," the Gunsmith reminded him.

"But Andy never came out of that swamp and I never heard anything about the Martels after that," Ryder declared. "If it wasn't for the fact that you're so damn famous and we kept hearing about the various adventures of the Gunsmith, I would have guessed you'd both perished in the bayou taking whatever secrets you knew about the Martels with you to a quicksand grave."

"Let's talk about that later, Chief," Clint urged. "I'm sure you've got enough problems with your current troubles in the city. You heard about that big gunfight at the harbor yesterday? A bunch of *apaches* and stevedores working for Gaston Lacombe were killed—"

"Oh, no," Ryder groaned. "Don't tell me you were involved in that."

"If you don't want me to tell you"—Clint sighed— "I won't."

"How the hell did you get mixed up with Lacombe?" the police chief demanded. "And why didn't you report this to me earlier?"

"Last night was pretty busy," the Gunsmith began. "But I'm ready to explain everything to you now if you'll just answer one question for me."

"I'm listening, Adams."

"Do you want Gaston Lacombe?"

"As badly as I want my soul to go to Heaven when I die," Ryder replied sternly.

"Okay." Clint nodded. "About a block from this station is a paddy wagon. Inside there are three members of your police department who have been on Lacombe's payroll for some time."

"Who are they?" Ryder demanded fiercely.

"You'll find out when we get there," Clint told him. "But we'd better hurry. The fella who's guarding them has a damn good reason to hate their guts because they conspired to murder his father. If we hang around here yapping all day, he'll probably start whittling on those three bastards with his cane sword."

"A cane sword?" Ryder raised his shaggy eyebrows. "What sort of a lunatic is helping you, Adams?"

"I'll introduce you," the Gunsmith replied. "Come on."

THIRTY-THREE

Chief Ryder followed the Gunsmith down the street. The paddy wagon was still parked by the curb, its team hobbled by thongs tied to their forelegs. Ryder marched to the rear of the wagon and reached for the door. Clint caught his arm.

"Not so fast," the Gunsmith warned. "My friend might blow your head off."

"He must be very nervous," Ryder commented.

"After what we've been through," Clint began, "you bet we're nervous. Marcel and I worked out a couple of passwords to be certain I'd be knocking at the door and he'd be inside with our prisoners."

The Gunsmith rapped his knuckles on the wagon. *"Merde* is French for shit," he declared.

"But shit is just shit in English," Marcel's voice replied as the door popped open.

"That was an odd choice for passwords," Ryder remarked.

"Yeah," Clint said. "But who would have guessed it?"

"Who would have thought of it in the first place?" Ryder muttered sourly.

The chief of police stared inside the paddy wagon. Marcel Duboir bowed in formal greeting. He held a revolver in one fist and his cane sword in the other.

"Bonjour, Monsieur Ryder,'' Marcel said as he shoved the gun into his belt.

"Good morning.'' The chief nodded. "Adams told me about your father, Marcel. I'm sorry. We all liked and admired Judge Duboir.''

"Not quite *all* of your men felt the same way,'' Clint corrected, tilting his head toward the three corrupt policemen inside the wagon.

The trio were securely manacled. Their hands were cuffed behind their backs and their ankles restricted by leg irons. All three had been gagged as well. Ryder's hard gaze fell on the lieutenant.

"Jean-Claude de Gasquet,'' he spat out the name as if the words caused a foul taste in his mouth. "I'm not surprised.''

"Oui," Marcel declared. "But de Gasquet has decided to share some valuable information with us.''

Marcel turned and suddenly thrust his sword at the floor. The sharp point of the blade pierced shoe leather and stabbed into de Gasquet's left instep. The crooked cop convulsed in agony, the gag muffling his attempt to shriek.

"Damn it, Marcel!'' Ryder snapped. "You can't torture those men—''

"But they can murder my father?'' Duboir hissed.

He yanked the tip of his sword from de Gasquet's wounded foot and raised the blade in a fast, graceful arch. The point caught the edge of de Gasquet's gag and adroitly tugged it from his mouth. It also sliced a bloody groove in the man's left cheek.

"Marcel'' Ryder cried.

"Relax, *mon ami;"* Duboir urged, but he held the sword ready, the point hovering less than an inch from de Gasquet's face. "The lieutenant wishes to talk to us.''

"Chief Ryder!" de Gasquet rasped fearfully. "Get these maniacs away from us!"

"If you do not tell us about your involvement with Gaston Lacombe," Marcel began in a voice that dripped icy venom, "I will slash this sword across your eyes. One quick move is all I'll need to slice one eyeball and gouge the other from its socket. If I manage to execute another sword stroke, I'll try to cut off as much of your penis and testicles as possible before Chief Ryder makes—"

"I'm warning you, Marcel . . ." Ryder began.

"And I warn *you, monsieur,*" Marcel snapped. "I am more concerned with avenging my slain father than obeying any of your laws. Do not interfere."

"He means it, Chief," Clint Adams told Ryder.

"You'd better talk to us, de Gasquet," the police chief said tensely.

"All right," de Gasquet gasped. "I've been working for Lacombe for almost two years. I've fed the syndicate information, helped them cover up crimes and altered investigations to conceal their activities."

"Wonderful" Ryder muttered.

"And we've got enough evidence to support his confession," Clint assured Ryder. "And we'll have even more after tonight."

"Why tonight?" Ryder asked.

"When I was taken prisoner by Lacombe's goons," the Gunsmith began, "Gaston stated that he intended to take care of the shopkeepers who oppose him. 'The resistance will go up in smoke tomorrow,' he said and he has half a dozen kegs of kerosene reserved for the occasion."

"There are shopkeepers opposed to Lacombe all over New Orleans," Marcel commented, jabbing his sword even closer at de Gasquet's face. "Where is the target area for this invasion?"

"I don't know . . ." de Gasquet began.

"Tell us or you'll need a white cane to find your way up the steps of the gallows so they can put a noose around your miserable neck!"

"Rue Trois!" de Gasquet cried.

"That's the street where Materott and the others have set up defenses against the *apaches*," Clint stated. "I helped them prepare and organize to fight the syndicate. Lacombe must be aware of this because I was obviously followed after I left Rue Trois."

"*Oui.*" De Gasquet nodded. "Gaston knows you have helped them. That is exactly why he chose that site. It is to serve as a lesson to other resistance groups. Gaston intends to prove that it is folly to try to fight him. If the others see that defenses are useless and that resisting only brings a terrible punishment of fire and death, the others will learn that the only way to protect themselves from the syndicate is to surrender to its demands."

"Well, your master will be in for a surprise, de Gasquet," Ryder declared. "When his *apaches* show up tonight, half the Department of Police will be waiting for them!"

"Not a good idea, Chief," Clint advised. "Lacombe had these three guys on his payroll. You don't know how many other police are secretly working for the bastard as well."

"Clint's right," Marcel agreed. "If you tell too many of your men about this, an informer is bound to get word to Lacombe and he'll cancel his plans for tonight. You'll have no idea when or where he'll strike instead."

"Maybe he's canceled the raid anyway," Ryder remarked. "After all, he knows that Clint heard his plans before he escaped last night."

"Maybe he has," the Gunsmith admitted. "But he

probably figures I wouldn't go to the police because they're infiltrated with informers. Besides, he wouldn't figure I'd have enough proof. All he knew about was the fact Marie and I escaped. It would be our word against his. With his City Hall connections, that wouldn't be good enough.''

"Especially since he planned to frame Clint for murdering my father," Marcel added.

"So there's at least a fifty-fifty chance he'll attack Rue Trois tonight," Ryder said. "And if he doesn't, we'll still have your testimony in court—as well as the girl's. Is Marie the Labou widow, by any chance?"

"I don't know if it's by chance," Clint replied. "But yes, she is."

"That might not work so well in court," the chief commented. "It's well known she blames Lacombe for her husband's murder. That could make her testimony suspect if Lacombe gets himself a smart lawyer—and you can bet your ass he will."

"Let's worry about a courtroom battle later," Marcel suggested. "The question right now is: How do we deal with him if he attacks Rue Trois?"

"Okay," Clint began. "First thing is we leave these three traitors in the paddy wagon until this is over. We can't have the entire police department knowing that de Gasquet and his pals were captured. Second, we'll need a handful of police officers we can trust."

"I can handle that part easily enough," Ryder declared.

"Make absolutely certain," the Gunsmith warned. "And don't get more than half a dozen."

"But Lacombe will bring a small army of *apaches!*" the chief exclaimed.

"He won't need that many to burn down some stores,"

Clint said. "Too many men could attract the attention of the local militia—just as too many cops heading toward Rue Trois will warn Lacombe's men that we're aware of their scheme."

"But I wouldn't have the men wear their uniforms or all arrive at the same time or from the same direction," Ryder stated.

"Still, too many men could ruin our plan," Clint insisted. "Criminals can spot lawmen pretty easy. The more police that show up, the more likely an *apache* will recognize the face of someone who arrested him in the past."

"Your plan had better be good, Clint," Ryder muttered.

"Well," the Gunsmith remarked, "we'll find out tonight one way or the other."

THIRTY-FOUR

By dusk, Rue Trois was a fortress. Clint Adams, Marcel Duboir, John Ryder and half a dozen New Orleans police officers in plain clothes had met with the local merchants. The shopkeepers were horrified to learn that their neighborhood had been chosen for an organized assault by Gaston Lacombe's syndicate.

Two families were too frightened to face the battle. They'd packed some baggage and fled. The others, however, were determined to stay and fight Lacombe. Fortunately, thanks to Clint's previous visit to the neighborhood, most of the preparations needed for the confrontation had already been made. After a few modifications of the local defenses, they were as ready for the invasion as possible.

The Gunsmith was experienced enough to realize that one can only prepare for a limited number of possibilities in a gun battle, but planned actions were seldom as important as being able to cope with the unexpected. Clint was a veteran of such confrontations. Marcel had proven he could handle himself in a tight spot, but what about the others?

The Gunsmith hoped the police were trained well enough to compensate for their lack of experience and the shopkeepers were frightened enough to follow orders and angry enough to fight like hell when the time came. Clint

Adams was skilled at many things, but forecasting the future wasn't one of his abilities. He simply accepted the reality of the situation and prepared to play out whatever hand Fate dealt him.

Clint just hoped it wouldn't be time to cash in his chips.

The *apaches* arrived at nine o'clock that night.

Four buckboards full of Lacombe's men appeared beneath the coal-oil light of the streetlamps. Two wagons rolled up to each end of Rue Trois as the *apaches* climbed out of the vehicles.

"Jesus," John Ryder rasped as he watched the hoodlums pile out of the buckboards. "There must be at least thirty of the bastards!"

The police chief was positioned in an alley with the Gunsmith and two New Orleans cops. All four men were armed with shotguns and rifles, except Clint who favored a revolver for close-quarters combat. However, since the fighting was apt to be pretty heavy, Clint had acquired an additional handgun besides his double-action Colt and the .22 belly gun. He also carried a .45 caliber Smith & Wesson Schofield with an eight-inch barrel. Clint wore the big pistol in a cross-draw holster on his belt.

"You told me Lacombe wouldn't send more men than he needed to burn down a few stores," Ryder growled, glaring at the Gunsmith.

"Reckon he figured that would take quite a few fellas." Clint shrugged. "You want to do something about them or just stand here and try to count them?"

"Let's get on with it," Ryder muttered.

The Gunsmith left the three policemen at the mouth of the alley and headed for the opposite end. He moved around the rear of a haberdashery and drew his Colt revolver. Favoring the shadows, Clint crept surreptitiously along the back of buildings, toward the west end of Rue Trois.

As he expected, the Gunsmith discovered four *apaches*. One rolled a wooden keg along the ground at the base of a grocery store while the other three held weapons ready. Clint would have been amazed if the arsonists hadn't chosen the blind side of the buildings for their destructive assault.

"You fellas are a little late to be making deliveries," the Gunsmith said softly.

"*Qui vive?*" a startled hood asked, wondering who confronted them.

"*Idiot!*" another man snapped. "*Abats le bâtard!*"

Before any of the *apaches* could try to 'kill the bastard,' Clint Adams opened fire. He ignored the man by the barrel and concentrated on the three escort members. The double-action Colt spat three rounds so fast the reports blended into one long roar of murderous thunder.

Three *apaches* tumbled to the ground. Two had been shot in the heart and the third man's skull had been drilled by a .45 round. The fourth and last member of the arsonist team abandoned the keg of kerosene and leaped for the cover of the nearest alley. He jumped between the grocery and a cobbler shop, yanking a pistol from his belt.

A gut-twisting scream of pain erupted from the alley. The *apache* staggered back into Clint's view. The hoodlum no longer had his gun—or the hand which had formerly held it. Blood gushed from the stump of his right wrist.

Marcel Duboir emerged from the alley, his cane sword in his fist. He snapped his wrist to flick the blood off his sword. Then a leg flew out in a high side-kick which hit the wounded *apache* in the chest. The man was forcibly propelled into the side of a brick building. He slid down the wall in a seated position, his head bowed in a dazed slumber.

"I thought you could use a hand, Clint," Marcel declared.

"So you took his, huh?" the Gunsmith remarked as he opened the loading gate of his modified Colt. "Keep an eye out for Lacombe's stooges while I reload."

Marcel drew his .44 Remington from his belt as Clint replaced the spent cartridges with fresh ammo. Police Chief Ryder shouted an order in French. Numerous guns snarled in reply.

"Our friend just asked the *apaches* to surrender," Marcel explained.

"And they refused," Clint added as he finished loading his Colt.

"*Oui.*" Marcel nodded. "In a rather universal language. Now what, *mon ami?*"

"If I have to explain it to you," the Gunsmith replied, "you should have stayed at home."

"*Touché.*" Marcel grinned. "And good hunting."

Rue Trois was a battlefield. Police and civilian defenders fired down at the invaders from windows and rooftops. A dozen *apaches* were cut down by the hail of hot lead before they could dash for cover. The thugs' guns cracked as the hoods scrambled for shelter.

Several members of the syndicate strike force picked the wrong place for cover. They charged into alleys where armed police and shopkeepers already lurked. The startled *apaches* found themselves face to face with the defenders. Guns roared and more bullet-riddled bodies fell.

One hapless hoodlum made the mistake of kicking in the door of a tannery. The owner was waiting inside with a

12-gauge shotgun. A blast of buckshot sent the *apache* hurtling back through the door. His mangled corpse tumbled into the middle of the street.

Clint Adams moved to the east end of Rue Trois. Two invaders had just hammered a wooden stake into the side of a keg of kerosene. They'd used wood instead of metal to avoid setting off any dangerous sparks around the flammable liquid. Then the hoods shoved the keg to send it rolling toward the nearest store.

Their plan was simple. The leaky keg would leave a trail of kerosene. One of the *apaches* would then toss a match to ignite the trail and the flame would burn a path to the keg which would strike the building and splash fiery destruction everywhere.

"Oh, shit!" Clint exclaimed as he broke into a full run.

The Gunsmith dashed forward to meet the fast approaching barrel. One of the hoods saw him and fired a poorly aimed shot at Clint. The bullet hissed past the right side of his face, nearly scarring his right cheek to match his left.

Clint didn't even notice the near miss. He concentrated on the keg which continued to roll closer. An *apache* tossed a lit match into the stream of kerosene left by the barrel. Flame immediately streaked forward.

The Gunsmith dove feet first at the keg. Executing a double kick that would have done justice to a *savate* expert, he struck the barrel with both feet. The kick sent the keg rolling back toward the two *apaches*. It rolled over the trail of fire, smothering most of the flame, yet a few sparks managed to ignite the keg.

The barrel burst apart, spewing flaming kerosene over the horrified *apaches*. Their screams pierced the sounds of gunfire and echoed into the night. Like two fugitive demons from Hell, the *apaches* stumbled blindly toward the Gunsmith, their bodies shrouded in crackling yellow flame.

Clint ended their suffering by pumping .45 mercy rounds into their charred flesh. The pair crumbled to the ground, tongues of fire still dancing on their remains.

The ominous triple click of a single-action revolver warned the Gunsmith of the threat which had crept up behind him. He pivoted to confront the *apache* who aimed a short-barreled pistol at Clint's face.

Suddenly the man's mouth fell open and a long, pointed blade jutted from it like a steel tongue. He was dead before he could pull the trigger of the cocked revolver in his fist. The corpse wilted to the ground and Marcel Duboir pried his cane sword from the base of the man's skull.

Marcel's smile of satisfaction vanished when he found himself staring into the muzzle of the Gunsmith's Colt. Clint squeezed the trigger. An orange comet burst from the muzzle and a bullet burned air inches from Marcel's left ear.

"Merde!" Duboir cried out as he recoiled from the Gunsmith only to trip and fall gracelessly to the ground.

Sprawled beside him was the object he'd stumbled over. It was the still twitching corpse of an *apache* with a fresh bullet hole between his open, lifeless eyes. Clint stepped forward and helped his friend get to his feet.

"Sorry to startle you," the Gunsmith explained, gesturing at the corpse with the smoking barrel of his gun. "But I had to get him fast before he got you."

"Oui." Marcel nodded breathlessly. *"Merci, mon ami."*

"Makes us even, pal," Clint replied.

The syndicate invaders were still trading lead with the defenders although two thirds of their group had fallen in battle. A few *apaches* were scattered among the alleys, desperately firing the last of their ammunition at the well-protected snipers who shot back from strategic positions throughout Rue Trois.

Five hoodlums had retreated to the two buckboards at the west end of the street, but they weren't planning to escape. The Gunsmith was already heading in their direction when one of the wagons bolted forward, pulled by two rapidly galloping, frightened horses.

No one was seated in the driver's position, but a long figure in the back was hunched low, pushing three kegs of kerosene from the speeding buckboard. The barrels tumbled into the street and rolled aimlessly. Sharpshooters on the rooftops opened fire on the *apache* in the wagon, their bullets nearly tearing him to pieces.

More rifle fire followed. The other hoodlums stationed at the remaining buckboard were using the rig for cover as they blasted holes into the three barrels of kerosene. The oily liquid oozed from the shattered containers to form a pool in the center of the street.

An *apache* struck a match on the side of the buckboard shelter and set fire to a bundle of rags tied to the end of a long stick. The Gunsmith approached as the man rose, about to hurl his torch at the kerosene puddle.

Clint shot the hoodlum in the chest, left of center. The bullet tore through the man's heart and blasted an exit hole under his shoulder. He collapsed behind the wagon, the torch still in his fist.

The trio of hoodlum riflemen shifted their weapons to try to draw a bead on the Gunsmith. Clint kept moving, dashing to the rear of the buckboard. He dove to the ground as the gunmen opened fire. Clint executed a fast shoulder roll and landed on one knee beside the dumbfounded *apaches*.

With his modified Colt in one hand and the S&W Schofield in the other, the Gunsmith seemed to have sudden death jutting from both arms. Forty-five caliber slugs crashed into the syndicate killers, drilling into their chests and smashing their faces like eggshells.

The shooting stopped. Clint saw several *apaches* emerge from alleys, their hands held high in surrender. The only conflict still in progress was between Marcel and a thug who wielded an empty Winchester as a club. Marcel attempted an overhead sword stroke at his opponent, but the *apache* raised his rifle to block it. The long blade struck the gun barrel and snapped in two.

Clint quickly tossed the S&W to his right hand and prepared to shoot the *apache* who swung a butt-stroke at Marcel's head. The agile Duboir, however, ducked beneath the whirling walnut stock and punched the broken sliver of his sword into the hoodlum's solar plexus. The *apache* dropped his rifle to claw at the blade buried in his chest. His mouth opened in a vain attempt to scream before he fell to the ground—dead.

The defenders of Rue Trois cheered in victory as they rushed forward to seize their prisoners. Chief of Police Ryder marched toward the Gunsmith, a wide smile plastered across his wide face.

"By God!" he declared. "We won! We've got enough evidence now to send Lacombe to the gallows twice!"

"Yeah," Clint agreed. "Providing the son of a bitch is still around when you try to arrest him."

Marcel strolled over to join them, his expression a mask of sorrow. "I broke my sword," he said sadly.

"You can buy another one tomorrow," the Gunsmith told him. "But we still have a little unfinished business to take care of tonight."

THIRTY-FIVE

The crew of *La Reine Rouge* were prepared for trouble. Stevedores and *apaches* patrolled the docks and the decks of the riverboat, all armed with shotguns or rifles. A Gatling gun was mounted on the port side by the gangplank.

"That bastard Lacombe must have found out what happened already," Chief Ryder muttered through clenched teeth as he gazed through the Gunsmith's pocket telescope at the boat.

"He's got a hell of a network of informers," Clint commented. "Nothing stays a secret from him for long."

Clint, Ryder, Marcel Duboir and three police officers had hurried to the harbor, hoping to catch Gaston Lacombe with his defenses down. Instead, they'd discovered *La Reine Rouge* was ready for action.

"I shouldn't have listened to you, Clint," Ryder complained. "We should have gotten reinforcements before we came here."

"That would take too much time," Clint insisted. "Lacombe's had a lot of furniture hauled off his riverboat. He's making the vessel lighter so they'll be able to get out of here fast."

"Clint's right," Marcel added. "And I haven't noticed that the crew is really very large. I've only counted seven men on board the boat and two patrolling the pier."

"Six against nine aren't exactly fair odds," Ryder stated. "Especially with that Gatling gun to deal with."

"Well, we need a good plan," the Gunsmith began. "One that—Give me that Dolland."

Clint had just seen two more of Lacombe's goons emerge from the cabin hold. They were dressed in striped pullover shirts and cloth caps, with pistols thrust in their belts, but the Gunsmith was more interested in the shapely young lady they were escorting down the gangplank.

"Baccarat," he confirmed when he gazed through the telescope. "I guess Lacombe figures she's excess baggage too."

"I admire his taste in luggage," Marcel mused.

"I'm going to go down there and try to talk to her," Clint announced. "Want me to introduce you, Marcel?"

"But of course." Duboir smiled. "She's beautiful and probably most charming, but do you think she can help us?"

"I sure hope so," the Gunsmith replied.

"Hold on, you two . . ." Ryder began.

"Not now," Clint told him. "We've got a boat to catch. You and your men wait here. If you see Marcel and me approach the boat, be ready to move in. You might have to take care of the guys patrolling the dock. Okay?"

"Damn it!" Ryder snapped. "I want an explanation. . . ."

But Clint and Marcel had already slithered away from their hiding place at the edge of the pier and hurried toward the dock.

The Gunsmith and his young French friend made the most of the cover available. Luckily, there were stacks of crates and piles of nets on the dock which served as excellent camouflage. Clint managed to keep track of Baccarat and her escort which had moved between two storage sheds. The Gunsmith and Marcel moved to it quickly. A man barked a harsh sentence in French.

"One of the *cochons* has ordered the girl to get down on her knees to service him," Marcel translated softly. "He seems to resent her."

"They ought to be preoccupied," Clint whispered. "Let's get 'em."

The Gunsmith and Marcel slipped between the sheds to find the two *apaches* with their backs turned to the pair. Baccarat knelt in front of the hoods. One man opened his fly and stepped toward her.

"*Suce moi, vache,*" he growled.

The other man giggled as he watched Baccarat take his partner's penis in her mouth. His laughter ceased abruptly when Clint Adams smashed the butt of his revolver on the top of the man's head.

The first thug crumbled with a groan. His partner quickly glanced over his shoulder to see the Gunsmith's Colt rocketing toward his face. A scream began to form as his mouth fell open, but the gun butt cracked into the point of his jaw before he could utter a sound. When the man fell unconscious at Clint's feet, the Gunsmith noticed the *apache*'s manhood was torn and bloodied.

Baccarat spat crimson. "We showed him, eh?" she remarked.

"Boy, did you show him," the Gunsmith agreed. "All I did was break his jaw."

"Gaston threw me out," Baccarat explained. "These two wanted to play with Gaston's discarded toy before they take off for the Gulf."

"Did you hear about what happened tonight?" Clint asked as he knelt beside one of the unconscious hoods.

"All I know is something has Gaston running scared." Baccarat laughed. "And I guessed that had to be you."

"How many men are on board that boat?" Clint inquired, pulling off the thug's shirt.

"Seven or eight," she answered. "Gaston doesn't intend to share with too many people."

"Good old greed," the Gunsmith commented as he stripped off his own shirt.

"You don't think you can just stroll on board because you change shirts with these baboons?" Baccarat asked in amazement.

"Lacombe's men are not so bright, *oui?*" Marcel remarked as he exchanged shirts with the other *apaches*. "And we'll only need the disguise for a minute or two. If it works that long, we'll be happy."

"You'll also be dead," she warned.

"Ah!" Marcel smiled, pulling on the hood's cap. "The lovely lady cares for me already. I must now survive, *ma cherie*, so I may return to you."

"Just stay put, Baccarat," Clint advised. "And keep your head down."

"And if either of these brutes begins to wake up, rap him in the head with this." Marcel handed her one of the *apaches'* guns.

"You're both crazy." She smiled. "I could probably fall in love with both of you. *Bonne chance.*"

THIRTY-SIX

"She's a wonderful girl," Marcel Duboir whispered as he and the Gunsmith walked across the pier. "When this is over—"

"Let's get it over first," Clint urged, tugging on the bill of his cap as they approached the boat.

"Oh, *oui*," Marcel agreed.

The pair walked past the two sentries patrolling the dock. Neither guard noticed anything suspicious about Clint or Marcel although they wore different colored trousers and Clint still carried his gunbelt with the Colt on his hip and the S&W in a cross-draw holster.

They quickly mounted the gangplank, expecting to hear a cry of alarm or a gunshot at any moment. None occurred, but the man stationed by the Gatling gun stared at them oddly. He asked Clint something in French. The Gunsmith merely shrugged.

"*Ce n'est rien à y voir*," Marcel told the *apache*.

The man turned to speak to Duboir. Marcel placed a hand on the closest rail and used it for a brace and threw his legs into the air. His right foot slammed into the guard's face with bone-breaking force. The *apache* fell to the deck, unconscious even before his head connected with the hard wood surface.

A voice shouted in alarm, but Clint ignored it as he quickly seized the Gatling and swung the barrels away from the dock to aim them at the other *apaches* still on board *La Reine Rouge*.

Two gun-toting figures charged forward. Clint turned the crank trigger of the Gatling. A metallic woodpecker of death rattled its lethal song and a volley of .44-caliber slugs chewed into the hoodlums. The impact of the multiple bullets kicked them across the width of the port quarter. They tumbled over the handrail and plunged into the water beyond.

"*Halte!*" Marcel shouted as he aimed his Remington at an *apache* who'd appeared at the bow.

"*Oui,*" the man replied as he raised his arms and tossed his Henry carbine overboard.

Clint glanced over his shoulder to see that Ryder and his cops had moved in quickly and apprehended the two sentries on the dock. Three more *apaches* arrived on the deck, but they held up empty hands in surrender.

"Over here," Clint pointed in front of the Gatling. "Marcel, tell those guys I want them over here so I can watch them."

"Certainly," Duboir agreed. "Then I'll hunt about to see if we have any more, *oui?*"

"Just be careful," Clint urged.

Marcel translated Clint's order into French and the four *apaches* marched in front of the Gatling, hands still held high. Almost immediately, Duboir found two more hoodlums who surrendered and tossed their weapons into the water as they joined the other prisoners.

"This is too easy," Clint commented nervously. *What the hell is Lacombe up to?*

"*Monsieur* Adams," one of the policemen began as he mounted the gangplank. "We have placed the criminals under arrest and—"

A pistol shot from the bridge cracked like a bolt of

deadly lightning. The bullet ricocheted off the steel frame of the Gatling gun. Another sniper opened fire. Clint heard the cop groan. His body tumbled down the gangplank like a bundle of lifeless clothes.

The Gunsmith swung the Gatling toward the hidden gunmen and cranked out a salvo of lead missiles. Two voices screamed and the enemy snipers bolted upright, their bodies shredded by rapid-fire bullets.

"Aw, hell," Clint gasped as one of the prisoners dove into him.

The unarmed *apache* had charged into Clint while his attention was on the two gunmen and the Gatling pointed in their direction. The Gunsmith, his assailant and the rapid-fire weapon all crashed to the deck. If the *apache* could just hold Clint for a second or two, the other five hoods would join him and stomp the Gunsmith to death before he could draw a gun.

Clint swung a knee into his opponent's ribcage to knock the man off balance. His right hand snaked out and caught the hoodlum at the back of the head. Clint shoved hard and drove the *apache*'s face into the wooden deck.

He gazed up to see Marcel Duboir boldly leap in front of the five advancing hoods before they could reach Clint. Marcel slashed a backhand stroke with the barrel of his Remington across one man's jaw. The *apache* fell, but one of his comrades suddenly kicked the gun from Marcel's grasp.

Marcel Duboir exploded into action like a whirlwind with fists and feet.

He immediately hooked a kick into a kidney of the man who'd disarmed him, followed by another kick with his other foot to the man's stomach. Marcel rapped his fist into the dazed *apache*'s face and then swung his first opponent into one of the other hoodlums.

The Gunsmith rose to his feet and prepared to draw his
Colt when another *apache* charged forward. Clint recognized the scrawny rat-faced hoodlum as the little thug
leaped into the air and launched a flying kick at the
Gunsmith's head.

Not this time! Clint thought as he simply stepped aside.

The man's foot missed its target. The *apache* was still
airborne, moving with the momentum of his own unsuc-
cessful technique. Clint yanked the S&W from its cross-
draw holster and chopped the revolver into the *apache*'s
back.

The little thug howled as the blow sent his still airborne
body hurtling over the top of a handrail. He sailed over the
edge of the pier and fell in a graceless, bone-bruising crash
on the merciless wooden dock below.

"Goddamn kangaroo," Clint muttered.

The Gunsmith turned to see Marcel was still fighting
with the other *apaches*—and winning. The young
Frenchman executed a low side-kick to a syndicate goon's
kneecap. The man stumbled and Marcel's other leg swung
in a high roundhouse kick to the *apache*'s head.

As the hood collapsed to the deck, another thug pulled a
knife from a belt sheath and prepared to plunge it between
Marcel's shoulder blades. Duboir barely glanced over his
shoulder at the *apache*. Then his leg shot backward,
driving a heel between the man's legs. The Lacombe hired
killer dropped his knife and clawed at his crushed genitals
as he wilted to the deck in a moaning heap.

Yet another *apache* tried a *savate* kick of his own,
trying to boot Marcel in the balls. Duboir's foot streaked
out and tagged the man on the shin before he could
complete the attack. Marcel then slammed a left hook into
the hoodlum's jaw and kept moving in the circular
momentum of the punch to ram a whirling side-kick into

his opponent's chest. The blow sent the man tumbling over a handrail to plunge into the water below.

"Jesus," Clint remarked. "He *is* crazy."

A small caliber pistol cracked and a bullet bit into a board near Clint's feet. He pivoted to see Gaston Lacombe at the bridge with a tiny .22-caliber Remington-Elliot derringer in his fist.

"You dumb shit," Clint hissed as he returned fire with the big Smith & Wesson.

A .45 slug splintered the wall of the bridge close to Gaston's position. Lacombe cried out in fear and ducked down out of sight. Clint dashed for the stairs leading up to the bridge.

"You're no good at trying to do your own killing, Lacombe," the Gunsmith shouted. "Throw out that peashooter and surrender before you convince me to kill you."

Gaston Lacombe, his hands raised, the Remington-Elliot in his right fist, stood out in the open on the bridge. Clint continued to mount the stairs.

"The gun, Lacombe," he insisted.

"*Oui.*" Gaston sighed as he tossed the derringer into the water beyond.

"Okay," the Gunsmith began, walking to the platform of the bridge. "Now, just come along . . ."

A huge figure suddenly appeared from the edge of the bridge compartment. Clint caught a glimpse of Jules's snarling face as the bodyguard seized his arm. Jules twisted the limb forcibly until the S&W fell from numb fingers.

"I'm glad *I* will be the one to kill you, *monsieur*," Jules hissed.

Clint glanced down at the giant's boots and realized Jules's left foot was closest. He quickly stomped the heel of his boot into the brute's instep. Jules yelped with surprise and pain. The Gunsmith hit him flush in the nose with an overhand left hook.

Jules replied with a right cross. The powerful punch knocked Clint five feet. He stumbled and fell, his head striking the floorboards of the upper deck. His jaw felt as if someone had sewn fragments of broken glass into it.

Through a blurry fog, the Gunsmith saw Jules march forward. The big man raised his right boot high and aimed it at Clint's head. The Gunsmith dodged the murderous stomp just in time. The steel foot stamped into the deck, cracking wood under its impact.

Clint braced himself on his shoulders and neck as he kicked out with both feet, scissoring his legs to trap Jules's leg. He twisted his body to the left and threw the startled thug off balance. Jules fell into a handrail and angrily stomped at Clint's legs with his left foot.

The Gunsmith had already released his scissors hold and scrambled away from the giant. He rose upright as Jules pushed himself away from the rail and launched another attack. The steel foot swung in a high roundhouse kick, aimed at Clint's face. He stepped back in time to avoid the whistling boot which smashed into the wall of the bridge cabin, shattering wood as if it were glass.

Jules yanked his foot free of the hole in the wall. Clint immediately snapped his own kick at the giant's crotch. The toe of Clint's boot slammed into Jules's testicles. The bodyguard groaned and bent slightly. Clint jabbed a fist into the big man's face.

A howl of pain and rage bellowed from Jules. Blood streamed from his broken nose. He dragged his steel foot more than he had before as he advanced. *My God*, Clint thought, *I'm slowly wearing him down!*

But the Gunsmith realized he was no match for Jules

He'd managed to avoid the steel foot thus far, but one kick would be all Jules needed to cripple or kill his opponent. Clint needed to put a little distance between himself and the bodyguard for less than a second. Just long enough to draw his Colt forty-five.

The Gunsmith backed away from the French behemoth and bumped into a metal object hung on a nail on the wall. He glanced at the bucket with FIRE painted in red letters on its frame.

Clint grabbed the bucket and hurled its contents at Jules's face in a single swift move. Sand hurled into the bodyguard's open eyes and mouth. Jules bellowed and pawed at his face.

The Gunsmith swung the bucket with all his might and brought it down on Jules's head. Metal crumpled over the giant's hard skull. Jules doubled up and Clint kicked him in the face. The blow sent him lumbering backward into the handrail.

Jules fell against the rail hard. His weight proved to be too great for the narrow wooden barrier. A portion of the rail broke away and Jules toppled off the bridge. He screamed briefly until he fell to the deck below. Clint drew his modified Colt and gazed down at his hulking adversary. Jules lay flat on his back, but his diaphragm rose and fell. He was only unconscious, surviving a fall which would have killed a normal man.

The Gunsmith turned to Gaston Lacombe. The portly syndicate boss calmly dabbed a silk cloth at his brow and shrugged.

"I see my ace in the hole wasn't quite good enough," he remarked.

"Game's over, Lacombe," Clint told him. "You lose."

THIRTY-SEVEN

Chief of Police John Ryder nodded his thanks as Marcel Duboir handed him a glass of brandy. The Gunsmith sat at a coffee table studying a disassembled revolver. Ryder strolled across the parlor and gazed down at the dismantled gun.

"What are you doing, Clint?" he asked.

"Trying to figure out how difficult it would be to alter this Smith & Wesson Schofield to fire double-action," the Gunsmith replied. "I've decided it would be a hell of a lot easier than it was to modify my Colt. I had to rebuild the entire frame of my Colt, but this Smith will only need to have the trigger mechanism altered, some work on the hammer and a couple of other simple changes to convert it for double-action."

"Well," Ryder began, "that's very interesting, but I thought you'd both like to hear what the district attorney said about Gaston Lacombe."

"Indeed we would," Marcel assured him.

"Lacombe and his henchmen have been charged with murder, conspiracy to commit murder, arson, attempted murder, kidnapping and blackmail," Ryder announced with a smile. "The D.A. says there's more than enough evidence to convict Lacombe and his crew on all of the above."

"So all of his men are in jail now?" Marcel asked.

180

"All except some of the small fry who will no doubt join smaller gangs and continue to be a problem." Ryder shrugged. "And a few of the *apaches* who are still in the hospital recovering from injuries you two gave them. The bodyguard Jules is one of them. Once they're well enough to be sent to prison, they'll get to wait for their appointment with the gallows along with Lacombe, de Gasquet and the others. The hangman will be very busy indeed."

"What about Lacombe's friends in City Hall?" Clint inquired: "Is there any chance they'll pull a few strings and get the bastard off?"

"None," Ryder replied. "We've already learned who they were. The mayor has 'encouraged' them to resign from office and leave the city. In fact, they've been advised to leave the state of Louisiana."

"I just hope they don't head out West," the Gunsmith commented. "We've got enough homegrown hootowls of our own without getting any imports."

"When are you leaving New Orleans, Clint?" Ryder asked.

"Not until we've paid a visit to *Le Café d'Amour*," Marcel announced as he slid a two-foot steel blade from his new cane sword. "After all, Clint is on vacation, *oui?*"

"Yeah," Clint Adams replied.

With the Lacombe syndicate out of action, the only thing that concerned the Gunsmith was which girl to see first—Marie Labou, Baccarat or one of the charming ladies at the café.

I wish all my problems were like this, he thought.

THIRTY-EIGHT

The giant limped across the lawn of the hospital, dragging his steel foot as he walked. Jules's breath was ragged and his lungs hurt. They'd applied a mustard plaster to his chest because he had three cracked ribs. His right arm was in a sling and his head bound with bandages.

Jules smiled coldly. The doctor had thought he was too badly injured to try to escape, but in the morning those fools would learn their mistake. *Oui.* In the morning they would start to search for Jules. This didn't worry the giant. He knew places in the city where he could hide until he healed enough to move on.

He knew he could not remain in New Orleans. Gaston Lacombe was ruined. Jules could not help his master now. Perhaps *Monsieur* Lacombe was doomed to die on the gallows, but his death would not go unavenged.

It would take time, Jules realized. He'd have to wait until his bones knitted and he recovered from his injuries. Clint Adams had been lucky, but Jules vowed the next time he met the Gunsmith, the outcome would be far different.

The man they called *L'armurier* had come from the West. From Texas, although Jules had heard that Clint Adams traveled a good deal. The West was very large and Jules was unfamiliar with the territory, yet he was certain he could find the Gunsmith. Clint Adams was a famous man and stories about him were plentiful.

The Gunsmith could not hide from his own reputation—and he would not be able to hide from Jules. When the time came, when he was ready, the giant swore to track down the Gunsmith and kill him.

Jules shuffled to the shadows beyond the hospital and limped deeper into the city. He had much to do, much to plan. . . .

But he had all the time in the world for revenge.

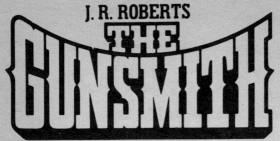

J. R. ROBERTS
THE GUNSMITH

SERIES

LONGARM

Explore the exciting Old West with
one of the men who made it wild!